Witching 1

Witch's Guide to

Romantic Comedy

Book 1

By Lotta Smith

Copyright

Witch's Guide to Romantic Comedy: Witching for Dante© 2021 Lotta Smith.

Cover copyright 2021 Molly Burton at CoverWorks

Editing and proofreading: Katie B. Thompson

All rights reserved.

No part of this book may be reproduced or transmitted in any form or by any means, electronic or mechanical, or by any information storage and retrieval system, without express written permission from the author/and publisher.

This book is a work of fiction. The names, characters, incidents and places are the products of the author's imagination, and are used fictitiously. None of the characters in this book is based on an actual person. Any resemblance to locales, actual events, or persons, living or dead, is entirely coincidental and an unintentional.

The author acknowledges the trademarked status and trademark owners of various products referenced in this work of fiction, which have been used without permission. The publication/use of these trademarks is not authorized, associated with, or sponsored by the trademark owners.

To hear about new books and discounted book sales, please sign up for my newsletter at:
Join my mailing list: https://amzn.us12.list-manage.com/subscribe?u=626844367df44e4c74176f268&id=79fab2b5cf
And follow me on Amazon: https://www.amazon.com/Lotta-Smith/e/B00VLM6FAU/

Previously published stories featuring the child version of Sophie:
Wicked or Treat!
My Wicked Valentine
Much Ado about Wicked Witness
Wicked on the Beach
All I Want for Christmas is Wicked
From Kyoto with Wicked
Summer Heat, Frozen Corpse, and Wicked

Prologue

"Ohh…!" Diving straight toward the floor, I squeak like a mouse with its tail trapped between a cat's fangs.

Locks of my hair fall across my face and obscures my view of the floor, which is now alarmingly close.

I'm Sophie Rowling. I'm twenty-five years old. Born in Manhattan, grew up in Kyoto, and currently, I'm living in Osaka, Japan. I have shoulder-length brown hair, brown eyes, and the motto of safety first. At the moment, I'm having the biggest crisis of my life.

I mean, this is such a big catastrophe. Probably even bigger than the time the side zipper of my dress popped open while I was on stage, exposing my boob to some 3,000 fans of classical music for approximately thirty-five minutes. The dress must have found that timing—the very beginning of the first movement of Tchaikovsky's Violin Concerto—

as the perfect moment to explode. Also, I forgot to put on my bra that night. But at least I was still able to play the violin as a soloist back then.

Anyway, in the middle of falling to the floor, I enjoy the luxury of stopping to worry about the impossible promise I made earlier—the promise to play the violin in front of my childhood teacher and classmates at a party just a month and a half away from now—while the fairy of my music skill has been taking a loooong leave, with no guarantee of coming back.

The abstract markings on the hard marble floor are growing larger and clearer by the nanosecond. In front of me, a tall tree is going down like it's leading my way. Just a second ago, I was hiding behind this potted plant, and now it's not covering me at all. Whoever said that everything is constantly changing was telling the truth.

Considering I'm so calm as I watch the floor approaching me—or rather, me coming closer to the floor—it looks like I could do something for damage control, such as stabilizing myself with my arms, but I'm doing nothing. I'm hesitant to risk hurting my hands or arms. I haven't completely ditched my hopes of playing the violin like I used to.

You may have already noticed…I'm clumsy. But in my previous life, I used to be a witch—or medium? Not so sure about the terms—so I used to cover my clumsiness by communicating with ghosts and fairies.

Anyway, I don't want to fall on my hands, so it's either going down face-first, or chest-first. Chipping my teeth and breaking facial bones doesn't sound all that lovely, so I brace myself to fall on my chest and stomach, hoping for the best, and for my body fat to minimize the impact. Thanks to living close to the gourmet shops and eateries serving yummy foods, I've been getting slightly heavier these days, but finally the extra fat tissue is likely to help me. Lucky me.

But again, like I said, strange things tend to happen around me.

While I'm bracing myself for a great fall with my arms up in the air and my head tossed back, a strong arm clasps me at the waist, scooping me up. In front of my eyes, a large hand grabs the falling tree by the leaves, stabilizing it on the floor.

"Hey, why don't you chill a little?" A low, deep, and cocky voice teases me. "Don't worry, baby. I won't bite you."

And the next thing I know, he's carrying me from behind, using only one arm. Depending on the situation, it could get really romantic, but it's not. Actually, the way he holds me resembles a dad carrying his little child.

I open my mouth, but I don't know what to say. What the hell is going on? Less than a minute ago, I was on my way to my workplace, back from an errand in Kyoto. I could have just gone home, but I decided to drop by the office and deliver my souvenir of yummy bread from the capital. Then I found my boss walking with a stranger. He was tall and muscular, probably in his late twenties to early thirties, and didn't fit my boss's clientele. She's Osaka's finest corporate lawyer. The man looked so different from my employer's clients. He was dressed too casually, and looked too hot and mysterious compared to other clients I'd met.

I have no idea what got into me, but instead of

saying hi to them, I hid behind a potted tree as they came toward me. In retrospect, I have no idea why I resorted to ducking and snooping. Then again, isn't it rude to sneak up from behind, startling me by talking to me when I least expect it?

"All right." The same voice goes on before I have time to complain. "I'll lower you to the floor nice and slow. So, don't wiggle or shriek. Is that clear?"

"Oh… Okay…" Mumbling, I nod many times.

I'm not very fond of his attitude, but at least he's true to his words. The next moment, my toes slowly touch the hard marble floor, and I'm on my own feet. "Whew… That was clo—"

He lets out a deep sigh, cutting off my monologue midway. "Holy crap. Who would have guessed it was a teenager who'd been staring at me so hotly?"

I narrow my eyes. What is he doing, touching me and insulting me? If I recall correctly, he's responsible for my stumble! I was just standing there in stealth mode, and he ambushed me, saying, "How can I help you, baby?" without even a warning, totally freaking me out. On top of all that, he's called me "baby" not just once, but twice.

"Stop calling me baby!" I turn back, snapping at him sharply. "Haven't you ever heard of—" I am so determined to make a point, but I trail off as my eyes register the navy jacket with a pinstripe pattern. My gaze moves upward until I come eye to eye with his beautifully sculpted face.

My jaw drops. Holy crap, he's the mysterious guy I saw with my boss!

The color of his eyes is an intense bluish green that reminds me of the Adriatic Sea. At the moment, these eyes are sparkling dangerously, prompting all the hairs on the back of my neck to stand up. As hot, gorgeous, and captivating as he is, there's something wild and savage about him. I've always felt that the actors starring as the heroes in the 007 movies don't live up to my kind of James Bond, but if this guy were to say, "The name's Bond. James Bond," I have a hunch I'd melt away like butter on a heated frying pan.

I move my focus way up to his thick, dark-blond hair styled in a low-fade pompadour, and…

Wow. He's so tall, probably even taller than my dad, who stands at 6'2". Then I notice this man's hair seems so much softer and velvety now that I have an up-close look. Without much thinking, I move my hand upward as if I'm trying to touch his hair and try its texture.

Then he clears his throat. "I have a little piece of advice for you, young lady." His tone is stern.

"A little piece of advice…for me?" I parrot, feeling like I've regressed to a child learning to speak. My hand stops moving.

"Yes." With a nod, he touches my jaw, tilting my face up.

I gasp, feeling terribly hot as if I've been transported into some kind of a sweat lodge. Under normal circumstances, my jaw would drop to the floor, but thanks to him holding my chin, it is still staying where it belongs.

"Never look at a random man like you're mentally undressing him and licking him all over. Guess what? Men lose control over much more trivial things than a glance that screams 'I want to fuck him!'"

"Fu… Wha…" I open and close my mouth, producing incoherent sounds. I don't know whether to be offended or embarrassed. On second thought, I might have been staring at him like a stalker, doing a little surveillance. "Um… I'm sorry. It might have been a bit creepy to watch you from the shadows… The thing is, I was having a hard time ripping my eyes away from you. Where are my manners? I don't usually stare at people, but you looked too hot to pass by. And…" Completely ignoring the smart part of me, my motormouth refuses to stop.

"You're so funny." A corner of his lips quirks up into a lopsided grin. As I shut up and purse my lips, he chuckles. "All right, now I'm tempted to give you a prize for honesty. Open your mouth, and I'll give you something sweet."

Oh my God! He's sooo going to kiss me! For a split second, I'm hesitant. I'm not familiar with kissing. To my dad's and granddaddy's dismay, I was a child who always rejected anybody's kisses, so I'm not sure if I can kiss like an expert. Besides that, the corridor of this office complex is rather crowded. More importantly, the office I work for is located at this property, and if someone I know sees me kissing this total stranger, how awkward would that be?

He's so right. I need to chill a little. So, I try to gain a little social distance between us by stepping back, but he lowers himself, with his bluish-green eyes studying my face.

"Wait a minute. It seems a little bit inappropriate to do that right here… And, full disclosure, it's gonna be my first…"

I trail off. Again. This time, something is inserted into my mouth between my open lips. As I shut up in total shock, it melts away in my mouth, a creamy, velvety sweetness with a hint of nutty flavor—of chocolate.

"The cashier at the café gave it to me as a complimentary gift, but I prefer something with a little more bitterness. Something more suitable for a grown-up." He winks, indicating the café he and my boss had come out from.

Savoring the chocolate while standing there like a total idiot, I wish I were dead. Or invisible, at least. Seriously, this is so embarrassing! What was I thinking? How could I make such a ridiculous assumption? Am I that needy?

"Save your dreamy stare for movie stars and royals, okay?" Raising his index finger, he smiles. "If you end up hooking up with a thug like me, your mom and dad are gonna cry."

A better woman would make a smartass remark or two, and a more pathetic woman would faint on the spot. I'm only myself, so I just manage to go with a lame, "Oh, okay," while pretending to still be savoring the rich, creamy aftertaste in my mouth. Honestly, my mind is blown, and I can't stop admiring his alluring grin.

"Good girl. Take care." His smile widens, and he gives me a light pat on my head.

"Wha—" I feel my face burn, and my heart is pounding like the cannon part in 1812 Overture. For a moment, I seriously wonder if I am actually dead, encountering an extremely sexy angel dripping with testosterone.

I shake my head, hoping to shed all the crazy ideas scattered in my brain. And the next thing I know, he's gone. Like, poof!

Looking around, I search for him with my

eyes, but I can't find him.

"Was he…real?" I mutter to myself. "Where are you, Mr. Almost James Bond?"

Chapter 1

A week later, I'm in my boss's office, sitting on the sofa, face-to-face with her.

"So, tell me, Sophie. What's been bothering you lately?" Megu Nakamura asks, with concern and kindness in her eyes. "You seem to have been pretty distracted for the past week or so."

"Well… I guess my focus has been a little bit shaky these days. I'm so sorry. That won't happen again," I say, and I mean it. I'm determined to restore my attention to my tasks while at work. The problem is, I have been pretty erratic, with tendencies to zone out while at the office. I know what's been affecting my concentration, but I just can't tell her about my obsession with the chocolate that mysterious guy threw into my mouth, right?

Seriously, I've got to get a grip. I don't want to disappoint my boss.

Megu is not just Osaka's finest lawyer and hot as hell. She's my boss, roommate, BFF, and guardian angel all rolled into one. When I first met her, she was a member of my legal team that swiftly rescued me out of a mess in Paris. When I met her for the second time, I was at the airport. Back then, my music career had just fallen into a coma, and Mom had decided to send me to the Gemological Institute of America's gemology school, insisting she heard a voice telling her to send her daughter to that program in Manhattan, and her daughter would be very talented in diamond and gemstone appraisal.

If you're thinking my mom's crazy, you're right. She talks to ghosts, fairies, and other spirits. I used to talk to them, but I stopped hearing such voices about the same time that my skill for playing the violin fell into a coma with no promise of ever waking up.

Anyway, I missed my flight, mostly because I didn't make it to the gate on time after spending too long trying out all the cool and fancy products at a smorgasbord of cosmetics counters between munching on gourmet local foods at the shops and eateries on the way. In Megu's case, she was simply late because of oversleeping, but we bonded at the gate after missing the same flight and commiserated with each other. Instead of joining the gemology school, I tagged along with her to New York City for her business trip. On the last day of her stay in the city, she asked me my thoughts about becoming her personal assistant and moving in with her.

I said, "Why not?" and came back to Osaka with her. A part of me was scared as I could imagine Mom getting really, really angry, like the times in my childhood when I used to lie about practicing the violin for the day.

Honestly, if you want to know what it's like to be frightened, you should try being at the receiving end of Mandy Rowling's fury. By the time my mom's done scolding the hell out of you, I guarantee you'll feel like half of your soul is sneaking out of your lips, trying to find somewhere safe. To my surprise, my mom was delighted to hear about my re-encounter with Megu and my altered plan. And I'm enjoying my new life, with its twenty-mile distance from my fussy, nosy parents and my bulky, noisy teenage triplet brothers.

Enough about my past. Let's focus on now.

"Did something shocking happen in Kyoto?" Megu looks into my face. "You've been distracted since then."

"Oh, no. Nothing happened there," I lie and skip the part about bumping into my childhood friends at Shimogamo Jinja shrine during my trip to Kyoto. Don't get me wrong, visiting the shrine was part of my task, as my boss wanted me to bring a talisman from the shrine to her. Of course I made a wish at the shrine, as the main deities residing there are famous for good fortune, success in one's career, victory, protection from all the evils, and restoration of one's power. In addition, I often visited this shrine in my childhood. When I was little, I used to live close to this shrine and Kamigamo Jinja shrine, and visited these shrines from time to time. Anyway, I always loved these sacred places and I didn't forget to visit Kamigamo as well.

On second thought, my wish was slightly related to the violin, so encountering my old friends there, asking me to play the instrument again might have been a sign. Anyway, I've got to either become able to play the violin as I used to in five weeks, come up with good, plausible excuses, ask some of my friends from my music college days to play the violin, or go with a quartet to entertain my first schoolteacher. But right now, I'm so obsessed with the mysterious guy I've nicknamed as Mr. Almost James Bond and his chocolate that I'm not going nuts worrying about the upcoming concert.

Seriously, that chocolate was so yummy. I mean, beyond delicious. It was sooo good and addictive. I wouldn't be shocked if it had been laced with some kind of drug. Just one taste and I'm already addicted. Considering that craving is the only lasting effect of the chocolate, its ingredients shouldn't be all that dangerous.

"Are you sure?" She tilts her head.

"Absolutely." I nod, wondering if it'd be a good idea to ask her about Mr. Almost James Bond. After all, she was with him, and she should know him. Then again, when he talked to her and patted her shoulder a week ago, she grimaced. I've been living and working with her for almost a year, and I know she's the queen of keeping a poker face. Besides that, when one of the younger lawyers at the firm had casually asked her about the rumor of this hunk seen with super-lawyer Nakamura, she denied it completely, saying, "I have no idea what you're talking about. If I were with such a handsome guy, I would be showing off a selfie or two taken with him."

I have no idea about my boss's intentions, but at least it's crystal clear that she doesn't want to talk about him. On second thought, her secrecy makes me even more curious about things, like the identity of Mr. Almost Bond and her relationship with him.

I've been obsessing about the chocolate with so much passion for the past week. Honestly, I'm growing concerned about my mental health. Due to the nature of Megu's business, my workplace has many visitors every day, and if anybody mentions those dangerous words like "the café on the lobby level" or "chocolates," my ears are all focused on them, completely forgetting about whatever I'd been doing just a moment ago. Sometimes, I find my hands shaking at the mention of these words. Am I turning into a junkie, or what?

With full disclosure, I visited that particular café and tried that complimentary chocolate, but it tasted different. The store manager was nice enough to sell me more chocolates with some begging, but none of them tasted as creamy or savory as the one he gave me. I went so far as to bulk-order the same chocolates, but again, they didn't live up to my standard. Following Megu's warning that we'd get sick if we ate all of them with just the two of us, I brought the big box of chocolates to the office so that all the employees here at Megumi Nakamura Law Firm, clients, and visitors like the delivery guys and the maintenance people can eat as much as they want.

The worst part about my obsession du jour is that I keep having a dream featuring this chocolate and Mr. Almost James Bond. I mean, every night, he returns to my dream in many shapes. Sometimes he's a bossy, arrogant, and insufferable CEO of some company I'm working for, and other times, he shows up as a law enforcement officer, such as the police and an FBI agent. One time he was a yakuza boss with his back, shoulders, and upper arms covered with ultra-colorful tattoos of a Japanese dragon, cherry blossoms, and a phoenix. And another time he was the boss of the Russian mafia. And every time, he seduces me, commands me to surrender, and then feeds me that chocolate… after warning me to never stare at a random man I'm not ready to… well, I mean, go the whole nine yards with.

Okay, perhaps I've been reading too many romance novels, and these books could be affecting my dreams, but these dreams are bothering me big time. One thing I do know, he's becoming more like Mr. Danger and Mr. Wrong.

As I'm mentally moaning and groaning, recalling the seductive vibes of Mr. Almost James Bond, Megu's face turns serious. "Please, Sophie. If you have any concerns, I can help. You know what? I offer discount rates for my loyal employees."

She looks ready to file some serious lawsuit, so I wave my hand in front of me. "It's not like that. Believe me, I'm staying away from trouble," sounding as if I'm always getting into trouble. I clear my throat. "Actually, I'm slightly worried about you."

"Pardon me?" She arches one of her perfectly shaped eyebrows. "Are you worried about me?"

"Well, actually, it's not you, it's me. I'm worried that I might have offended you by committing some serious error," I confide. "I might be overreacting, but ever since your return from the U.S. trip, it feels like you're hiding something from me. Of course, I fully understand that confidentiality is very important… But, can you at least tell me what I did wrong? I'll be extra careful not to make the same mistake, and…" As I speak, I get a really heavy feeling in the pit of my stomach. I know I lack the expertise to work as a lawyer's assistant, but recently, she's been taking the calls that I used to handle as the middleperson. In retrospect, it feels like she sent me to Kyoto for an errand, just to get rid of me for a day and a half. The document I delivered wasn't urgent, and the client was pretty surprised that I'd delivered it in person.

"Come on, Sophie, you're overreacting." She chuckles, flashing her perfect set of pearly whites. "You've been doing great work for me all the time, and I appreciate you so much. And, you know I'd be openly complaining to you if I found your work unsatisfactory."

"That's a good point." I nod. Her straightforwardness is one of the many things I like about her.

"You know that I represent Kakubeni Holdings?"

"Oh, sure," I agree with her, but I feel my heart beating faster than normal. Kakubeni is a huge trading company in Japan, and they're a part of the trouble that hit me and killed a part of me in Paris.

"Actually, my latest trip to the States was for Kakubeni, and this case happens to be more private than my usual cases. Instead of the company, the CEO himself has hired me to represent him in the U.S.," she explains, massaging her temples. "The global trading division of Kakubeni had a contract with a U.S. company, without going through the processes for approval by the board members, completely breaking protocol. Can you believe this? Just one employee of that division did that."

"That doesn't sound too good," I comment.

"That's the understatement of the year." She shrugs. "Shortly after making that contract, it turns out that their vendor has some major issues to work with. And, that's where the CEO stepped in, hiring me. My job is to cancel the contract as soon and smoothly as possible. I didn't tell you about my job with Kakubeni, mostly because I thought you wouldn't be thrilled about visiting their headquarters and so on—even if the division I'm working with is different from their culture promotion foundation."

I try to come up with something smart, but I only manage not to start shaking like a junkie. I breathe slowly, trying my best to delete the haunting image of a shattered Stradivarius.

Kakubeni Holdings' culture promotion foundation happens to be very much related to the mess in Paris, where my violin career went into a coma. They were the owners who used to lease a Stradivarius to a certain guy who was a celebrity musician. Except, this violin is dead for good, and they accused me of killing the king of all the violins and their favorite star.

To make it worse, the police department in Paris found me knocked out in the star's suite at the five-star hotel; the star had dropped dead before raping me. Just because they discovered me at the same suite with a dead star and a splintered Stradivarius, they accused me of murder. Haven't they ever heard of this saying, "Once a violinist, always a violinist?" A violinist would never use a violin, especially a Stradivarius, as a murder weapon. Come to think of it, the suite had chairs, wine bottles, and heavy ashtrays. What kind of idiot uses a historical violin masterpiece worth 3 million dollars? Besides that, the cause of death was electrocution. Somehow, he was found scorched to death—as if he was hit by a thunderbolt. My parents and granddaddy were talking about cases of spontaneous human combustion, concluding that it's not seriously weird for the star to be electrocuted with no known cause.

The worst part is that I went deaf and blind after the mess.

Not physically, but mentally. Ever since that catastrophic night in Paris, I haven't been able to see or hear Jackie and Allegra.

Anyway, if it were not for Megu and the rest of my defense team my dad and granddaddy had hired, I could be rotting in a gross jail cell infested with mice and lice. When I used to tour outside of Japan, my fellow musicians used to call me Sophie the Fussy and Sophie with OCD, but in my honest opinion, it's so abnormal to see mice and lice in the heart of the nation's capital!

"Honestly, if only they A-bombed Paris instead of Hiroshima and Nagasaki back in 1945, the new, current Paris would be a cleaner, nicer, and better place… Something that lives up to the reputation as the City of Light… not the city that stinks, littered with poop…" I mutter, not noticing that I'm saying it aloud.

"Sophie, I agree with you that Paris is one of the filthiest places on the earth, but don't go out telling what you've just said, okay? I'm pro-free speech, but some things are better left unsaid." Megu moves her index finger like the windshield wiper.

"Oh, of course." I nod many times and zone out, again. On second thought, this could be a great opportunity for closure, and… "You know what? France has many great craftsmen, so keeping Paris as it is might not be bad, as the place works as some sort of showroom, at least. By the way, Megu, I'm a professional, and I'd be more than happy to work with any clients."

"That's great to hear." She smiles. "But the

main reason for my secrecy is something else. Like I said, it's a private gig rather than an official corporate case. This particular employee who rushed contracting with a not-so-trustworthy vendor happens to be the son of the CEO. It's customary for the majority of companies in Japan to hand over the business to a blood heir, but lately, things aren't so simple, with shareholders having a bigger say nowadays, compliance, and blah, blah, blah. Anyway, the rumor is that he rushed in to this arrangement, trying to solidify his ground to become the next CEO."

"Oh…" I'm itching to comment that this CEO's son's attempt seems to be backfiring, but I hold my tongue. As a professional, I shouldn't diss my boss's client. If I recall right, this son of the CEO is still twenty-something, as he was born when the CEO was in his mid-fifties. The CEO himself is known for the charisma and brilliance in business, but the rumors are that the board members are pretty skeptical about handing the company over to the young son of the CEO.

"So, this case is more like a faux-pas than a

crime. Then again, depending on the perspective, it could be less damaging if that stupid boy had actually committed a crime. My job is all about damage control, with my client requesting the highest level of secrecy. That's why I've been rather stealthy these days. So, just relax and rest assured, okay?"

"Sure." I let out a sigh of relief.

"I think I'll be traveling to the U.S. sometime in the near future to work on this case."

"Okay, then I'll book the flights and so on."

"I'll let you know when I have the exact date from my client." She stands up and gestures for me to stay seated. "Actually, there's a task I need your help with."

"Oh, of course. Consider it done." I perk up.

She pulls an envelope out of her desk drawer and hands it to me. "There you go. Can you deliver it to a certain person?"

Chapter 2

About an hour later, I'm sitting on one of the cushy sofa sets in the lobby of the Phoenix International Hotel, a five-star hotel that opened earlier this year in Kitashinchi, one of the hippest areas of Osaka.

My mission is to deliver the envelope to the hotel's front desk, nothing more or less. According to Megu, she's already contacted the hotel, so I should be able to drop the envelope off and leave immediately. My boss was secretive about this errand as well, making it crystal clear that nobody at the firm should know that she sent me to the hotel in the first place. Still, now that I know the reason for her secrecy, my initial worries have faded away.

To be honest, I'd rather be visiting the gourmet shop that I passed by on the way, browsing all the cute and yummy-looking goods from the deli menu to sweet delights. Except, when I was about to hand the envelope to one of the staff at the front desk, she asked me to wait in the reception area, saying that

Mr. Walker has requested that the delivery be handed to him in person. Now that I have learned the name of the recipient for the first time, it feels a little bit awkward. I didn't pepper my boss with questions because I fully understood her tricky situation, but now I can picture Mr. Walker as an old, fussy, and persistent dude with deep frown lines engraved between his eyes.

Checking the time on my phone, I'm itching to finish the job and visit the gourmet shop. With the stomach-churning concerns dissolved into nothing, I'm in the mood for a little bit of a treat—such as chocolates with creamy fillings. Speaking of chocolates, my obsession with Mr. Almost Bond's chocolate hasn't faded yet, but if I come across something extremely delicious, I might be able to rewrite my memory of the yummiest chocolate I've ever tasted, and move on.

When I try to put the phone back inside the purse on my lap, the whole thing, including the envelope, falls onto the floor. Good thing the surface is covered by thick carpet. "Oopsie… That was close. Good thing the cranky Mr. Walker hasn't arrived yet.

He's so late to come. Maybe he has prostate trouble, taking forever to pee." Mumbling and chuckling to myself, I bend down to pick up the stuff.

And the next moment, I notice a sheet of paper slipping out of the now open envelope. I try to push it back with the speed of light, but I can't stop reading what's written on it. It looks like a check, with the name of a U.S. bank that I don't recognize, signed by Megu herself. My eyes widen as 300,000 printed after the dollar sign registers in my brain. If you're looking for a violin, $300,000 will get you a decent piece, and actually, this sum of money is good enough to buy you a rather sizable detached home in the suburbs in Japan.

What is my boss thinking? That's a crazy amount of money to let her PA handle. But at least it tells me that she trusts me enough to manage a large amount of money.

At the same time, the knowledge that I've inadvertently witnessed the contents of the envelope, and uneasiness seeps into my skin. What if the reason she told me to just drop it at the front desk was to keep me from encountering this Mr. Walker? One minute ago, he was just a little grumpy old man, but now he's turning really dangerous. What if he's in some kind of a mob? Even worse, an assassin? Speaking of an assassin, there was a time when Mr. Almost James Bond starred in my dreams as a super-sexy assassin seducing the heck out of me...

Enough with my obsession! My gut instinct is screaming like a banshee, shrieking that staying here and waiting for the mysterious Mr. Walker was a big mistake. I should have just shoved the envelope into the front desk staff's face and run like hell. I've already had my life's share of trouble and trauma in Paris. I failed to run when that star virtuoso used "Something's missing in your music... something that can't be covered with technique—even for a marvelous musician like you" as a pickup line and ended up losing not only my career but a crucial part of my family. I'm not making the same mistake again. Been there, done that. No more trouble for me, thank you very much.

My mind is set. I'm not making the same mistake of being influenced by others. This time, it might cost me even bigger, such as getting killed by an ax murderer. On second thought, if I die and become a ghost, I might be able to talk to Jackie and Allegra again, but the backrest of the sofa makes a snapping sound, grabbing me back to reality.

I stand up, ready to run to the front desk and shove the envelope and leave here. But...

"Hey! Leaving here immediately after sneaking a look at what's inside the envelope? How classy is that?" a deep, bass-baritone talks to me. "Apparently, Nakamura needs to hire somebody less shady."

"No speak English! *Watashi, eigo wakarimasen*!" I snap in Japanese, using the clueless card. Good thing the official language here is Japanese. I'm not changing my plan just because somebody said really rude and obnoxious things in English. Ha! Definitely, he's such an asshole, holding one of my shoulders with his large hand. I shake off his hand, muttering "*Oitaga sugiruto minasan okoriharuwa,*" with the superficial meaning of "If you keep on behaving like that, people will get angry with you," which actually means "I'm angry with your obnoxious behavior!" Guess what, Japanese conversation is all about subtlety.

"Come on, is this smartass brat the best she could hire?" He chuckles, switching the language into Japanese. "Talk about lacking respect."

"A brat? Excuse me? Where's that brat? Didn't your mom teach you that if you want respect from others, you've got to treat people with courtesy? Oh, did I mention I'm just doing my job because I'm supposed to drop this envelope at this hotel's front desk? By the way, aren't you a tad bit blunt yourself for someone who wasted my ti…" I trail off as I turn back to face him, ready to hammer the last nail into the coffin called my greatest rant in English.

He's tall, muscular, and… suave. Very suave. He looks like the mysterious Mr. Almost James Bond that I've been obsessing about for the past week… The dark blond hair, the sharp lines outlining his cheeks and jaw, and the strong physique like one of those statues of Greek gods—unless he has an identical twin, triplets, or quintuplets, he should be Mr. Almost Bond himself.

I take one more step toward him and look up at him. Oh, yeah, my neck's stretched in the same angle as the last time I looked up at Mr. Almost Bond. I take a mental note that his name is Mr. Walker. I need a little more info to solidify my theory. He's sporting a pair of dark shades, and I can't see his eye color. "Can you take off your shades for a moment? You look very much like somebody else I've encountered lately."

Without words, he takes off the sunglasses and lowers himself, looking into my face.

I stop breathing for a split-second, overwhelmed by the bluish green. Probably due to the lighting, the color of his eyes looks more intense than it used to be a week ago.

"What a shocker." He tilts his head to the side. "Who could have imagined you're the same girl hiding behind the greens?"

"I'm impressed with your memory." I shrug.

"That's interesting. So, you're the staff Nakamura has sent here? You're a teenager, aren't you?"

"I am not! I'm twenty-five years old!" I snap at him. "I might be just five feet two inches tall, but…"

"Your bra size is like thirty-four double-D, with the waist around twenty-seven," he observes.

"WHAT?" I gasp. Why does he know my size?

"Gotcha! I'm right." He grins. "As for the weight, it'll be something like—"

"Stop that! That's sexual harassment!" I squeak in panic. "I'm gonna sue the hell out of you!"

"Oh, yeah? Wow, it looks like I've gotta hire Counselor Nakamura, one of the best lawyers in Japan," he responds with a joke, as if he's completely enjoying the situation.

Biting my lower lip, I'm busy making the strategies for my next moves. I don't like his cocky attitude. I can't believe I'd been obsessing about him for the past week! But, wait a minute, who the heck is he? It's not normal for Megu to hand over a check written for $300,000, right? All right, I need to obtain a little more information so that I can have a closure and move on. Taking a deep breath, I say, "Mr. Walker, I have a question."

"Dante," he corrects. "Call me Dante."

"Dante?" I hesitate, but say the word aloud

anyway. Why am I salivating?

"Yup, my friends call me by my first name." Casually, he clips his shades on the breast pocket of his white linen shirt, looking as if he's popped out of some movie. On this day, he seems like he's ready to hop on a yacht, completing the look with washed out jeans and deck shoes.

"Oh… really?" I mutter almost to myself, trying my best to sound unimpressed.

"And, your name is?"

"I'm Sophie Rowling… Wait a minute." I frown. "Technically, it's not like we're friends, and…" Is it even safe to let him know my full name in the first place?

"Sophie. What a lovely name. So, Sophie, are you a lawyer yourself?" He perks up, casually addressing me by my first name. With full disclosure, I'm feeling a little bit tickled—mostly because it's more common to be addressed with the family name here in Japan, unless I'm talking to a very close friend.

"I'm just an assistant to Counselor Nakamura…" Wait a minute, why is he taking the lead of this conversation?

"Oh, okay, you're a paralegal." He's talking so nonchalantly I can't help but feel a sting in the heart.

I clear my throat. "Um… I'm not a paralegal. Actually, I've never studied law, and I'm just an… assistant."

"What's the matter?" He studies me. "Why are you looking so… What's the word? Sad? Embarrassed? Or, confused? Hell, it's hard to express in Japanese." Slightly shaking his head, he switches to English. "Am I responsible for you looking like you're about to burst into tears?"

I don't answer him, mostly because I can't. All of his words are right. I'm sad and embarrassed for my lost career, and I'm still dazed and confused about what to do with my life. Everybody close to me says that what's keeping me from playing the violin like I used to is only psychological, and I'll come back as a greater, better violinist. Then again, nobody knows when that will happen.

Mrs. Taniguchi, one of the professors under whom I studied back in college, who's likely to win the gold medal for being the most awed and feared teacher, had once stormed into the lesson room where I was making shaky, irregular, and disastrous noises in the name of rehabilitation. She demanded to know who the heck was making such terrible noises. The teacher helping with my rehab program displayed an ambiguous smile to avoid answering her. I mumbled something about my shaky performance ever since the *accident* in Paris. Then Mrs. Taniguchi barked at me. "Stop mumbling your lame excuses about the dead super-star or the shattered Stradivarius already!

"Guess what? I would cry for you if it were *you* who was found dead, or if it were *your violin* that got damaged beyond repair. Newsflash! You're alive, physically able to do whatever you wish to, including but not limited to playing the violin like the virtuoso you used to be. What's more, the dead Stradivarius wasn't yours to begin with! Stop being so lame and apologetic like a total loser! Of course, it's a shame to lose such a historical piece, but nothing is unbreakable. I'm sure the idiots from Kakubeni are laughing their asses off, getting a huge sum of insurance money, along with so much media coverage.

"The next time anybody harasses you about the Stradivarius, just say something like, 'I feel terrible about the violin... If only the owner had leased it to someone who handled it with better caution and more responsibility, it would be still alive. So sad that such a historical piece committed suicide to save the future virtuosos from the evilness of its temporary owner.' Besides that, the super-star who drugged you that night turned out to be a serial *rapist* with a track record of crushing young talents like mosquitos before they blossomed in full. Your eyes are gonna roll out of your head if you look at the number of sexual harassment and assault allegations against him after his death. A lot! I mean, dozens, at least. Could be over a hundred. History will remember you as the hero who made the world a better place by sweeping the bastard off this world. Like it or not, you're gonna play the violin because it's not just about your career, it's one of the largest parts of your life! Remember, I've never mentored a loser, and will never do so. You will make a comeback. Or else the world itself is as good as finished.

"On the plus side, you're having your first ever long vacation since starting your professional career at the age of nine. This kind of sabbatical is God-given, so enjoy your time off while you can. You'll thank me later."

Who said music teachers can't give a pep-talk like one of those football coaches? Since then, I've been feeling better, but my arms are still sloppy and my fingers are shaky whenever I hold the violin. Speaking of playing the violin, what should I do about the little concert for my teacher from the first grade?

As I freeze, muttering, "Gotta enjoy my long vacation while it lasts…" a large hand touches one of my cheeks. "Don't take my words so seriously, please. I was just guessing," His touch and tone are deceptively gentle, but… "For a woman who tried to steal a $300,000 check, you're so sensitive."

I slap his hand off. "I said I was just delivering it! Are you deaf or what?" I glare at him, trying to read his mind and determine his identity. After all, my personal errand for Megu has been full of irregularities so far, so I have to be really careful. Except, I'm no psychic, and staring at him gives no answer.

And the next thing I know, he cracks up laughing. "Oh, yeah. It's good to see your smartass side coming back."

Holy moly… my heart is melting like an ice candy left under the scorching sun in the middle of summer.

I look at the envelope in my hand, and then at Dante. I'm here for an errand, after all. I'm about to hand him the item, but then it hits me that I'm about to screw up again. "Look, Counselor Nakamura made it crystal clear that I was to deliver this to the front desk of this hotel. I have no information about the recipient's name or room number, so I can't just hand it over to you. What if you happen to be a swindler out to steal this check?"

He lets out a deep sigh. "Look at the check. My name should be written on it."

I check the inside, and Dante Walker is written on it. "You need to prove that you're the real Dante Walker."

He whistles. "Wow. You're a tough cookie. All right, let me show you my passport... Shit, it's still in my bag. Can you come to my room?"

I'm tempted to nod okay, but I knit my eyebrows. Isn't it a red flag for rape or murder? If I'm found dismembered in the hotel's bathtub, I don't have to worry about my future, including my music and everything, but I'm not thrilled about this option. Having been discovered passed out and drooling was humiliating enough, showing my innards to the hotel staff and maybe the police is so going to kill me with embarrassment.

"I have an idea." I'm trying to keep my tone cool and composed, and so far, so good. "Let's go to the front desk and have the staff convince me."

"Seriously? What if I'm a thief staying here with an alias?"

"What?" My jaw drops. That was a possibility that I didn't even imagine.

While I'm starting to freak out, Dante is pretty cool and relaxed. "Oh, okay. You're afraid of visiting a man's room. Apparently, you're one of those girls who's never been alone with the opposite sex, except for your own family members."

"Excuse me?" I narrow my eyes at him. Seriously, he's getting on my nerves! I'm so desperate to shoot back at him that I blurt out something unexpected. "Not every woman is attracted to men. Actually, Counselor Nakamura and I've been living together, alone at her condo, for about a year. You know what I mean? It takes a little bit of romantic attraction to continue such a living arrangement."

Oh my God… I can't believe I've just spilled such a blatant lie…

I'm mentally blanching like a panty soaked way too long in bleach, but at least I am trying my best to look breezy. For a moment, Dante's face looks serious, but immediately, the cocky grin comes back on his face.

"I get your point. I guess you'd want to come to my room. After all, we're talking about a lot of money, a transaction with your *partner*." He emphasizes the p-word, "Don't you think it'd be safe to check the recipient's identity, at least?"

"Oh, yes…" I mutter. "I've got to watch over

my partner's transactions…"

Liar, liar, pants on fire… Feeling the flames of hell scorching my bottom, I have no choice but to tag along with him to the upper floor. Mom used to tell me that lying through my teeth would eventually get me into trouble, and she was sooo right.

Chapter 3

The room Dante's staying in turns out to be the presidential suite at the top of the high-rise hotel.

The entrance door opens to a spacious living room with floor-to-ceiling windows overlooking the stunning city. The décor is so modern and sophisticated, like I've wandered into some sort of museum. If I recall correctly, some of the suites offer stunning views, like Hep Five with their signature red rooftop Ferris wheel. I imagine the night view from the bedroom must be even more fabulous than the one I'm looking at right now.

Not that I'm going into the bedroom or staying here until night. Just because I've walked into the suite doesn't mean I can't leave here in one minute or so, right? Okay, I could have waited outside the room, but it's my first time to visit this hotel, and, well… I don't mind taking a little suite tour provided by the mysterious Dante Walker. Who wouldn't like taking a sneak peek at a newly-opened gorgeous hotel?

As he says, "Help yourself," I'm standing close to one of the windows, taking in the scenery, I notice this view seems somewhat familiar. Not just familiar, it feels like I've seen this view over and over. Wait a minute. My eyes widen. Isn't it the same room that I've repeatedly seen seeing for the past week? Oh my God... this is the room where Dante, formerly known as Mr. Almost James Bond, seduced me every night... Okay, technically, everything happened only in my dream, so it's nothing I should fuss about, haha...

So, everything that I believe has happened must have been a factor of my dream. Getting up in the morning, having a little chat with Megu, and visiting Phoenix International for an errand, and reencountering Mr. Almost James Bond... these are all pieces of my wild imagination. My heart starts to beat faster, and I wonder if I'm even alive. What if I am already dead and the reason I can't properly play the violin happens to be because I've already turned into a ghost? On second thought, if I were a ghost myself, I should be able to talk to other ghosts and maybe fairies, such as Jackie and Allegra.

Okay, Sophie. No need to panic. It's just another weird dream featuring Mr. Almost James Bond... Take a deep breath and close your eyes and go back to sleep...

I close my eyes, following the voice of reasons a-blasting in my head. Immediately, the widespread skyline of the city disappears. So far, so good. Who could have imagined it's possible to shut your eyes in the middle of a dream when you're fully asleep?

And the next thing I know, the deep, broad, and seductive voice brings me back to reality.

"What are you doing, Sophie? Don't tell me you're playing the ostrich burying its head in the sand." I resist him by completely ignoring him, but he has the audacity to add, "Holy shit. I've never seen someone actually using this tactic. Honestly, you never cease to amuse me, baby."

"I'm not a baby!" I snap back, reopening my eyes. "My name is Sophie Rowling, as I told you just minutes ago. Are you demented or what?" Then I check out the place, moving only my eyes to find out that I'm still in the same suite with the same décor and scenery I've seen many times.

"Demented? Who, me?" He chuckles, taking a step toward me. "Look at the view. Isn't it stunning? On second thought, you're accustomed to seeing a prettier sight from your partner's place, right? If I recall, Counselor Nakamura's residence is located in a high-rise condo, right?"

"Um… yes. Her condo is on the thirty-fourth floor… so it feels slightly higher here at the thirty-seventh floor," I reply.

"So, you two live in the building right next to the one with Nakamura's firm. Commuting must be so easy for you ladies. By the way, do you still think I'm demented?" Along with him asking playfully, I feel his presence coming even closer to me. And the moment my eyes catch one of his strong arms, both of his hands are pressed on the window—practically caging me in him.

"So far, it seems like you have good memory," I mutter, knitting my eyebrows. "By the way, have you heard of social distance?"

He doesn't answer, but he's so close that I feel his heat at the nape of my neck. Indeed, he's so close to me that the back of my sensible knee-length pink dress is brushing against him. If I take one step behind, my head will bump into his broad chest.

"Um... Hello? Mister... I mean, Dante... *san*?" A little piece of Japanese language slips out. *San* is a very convenient, universal word to add a little respect to someone you talk to. It works for just about anybody, regardless of their gender, age, and social status.

"Seriously?" He snorts out over my head. "You're the first person to address me like that. Oh, now I remember, you're someone who calls your partner Counselor Nakamura."

My heart jumps. "I'm a professional. I can't be so familiar with her at work."

Do I rock at being convincing, or what?

"How do you address her outside of your professional relationship?" he presses on.

"Megu," I answer. It's good to say something without worrying about getting caught lying.

"What is she like in bed?"

"What!" Caught in total surprise, I gasp. I might have jumped a little bit, and as a result, I lose my balance—again. In an attempt to regain balance, I grab for anything within my reach, which turns out to be his arm. "Oopsie, sorry." Feeling so awkward, I wish I was invisible.

"I see." He chuckles knowingly. "Is that your typical method of seduction?"

"Hyet!" I let out another gasp. "I… I… I don't know… what you're talking about…" Apparently, I'm in deep trouble. There's an alarm blasting in my head to run like hell, so the first step is getting more distance between him and me.

He grabs my wrist before I can manage to move. "You're the one who said that you've been living with her for about a year, with romantic involvement and everything."

"Hey, what are you doing?" I squeak in a trembling voice, but his grip doesn't loosen up. Oh my God… If he breaks my arm, I'll end up being physically unable to play the violin… for good… And the next thing I know, I'm pleading, "Please don't break my arm. If you want to get really rough, you can just rape me, but don't hurt my arms, back or legs…" I don't tell him that the guy who attempted to rape me the last time ended up dead before he could even undress me.

"Did you tempt her? Or has she turned into a pedophile lesbian?" Completely ignoring me, he presses on.

"Stop being irrational… If you keep on doing this, I'll sue you like hell…"

"This is important. Depending on your answer, the figure written on the check will significantly change." He's still trapping me in his arms, but his clasp isn't as tight as it was in the beginning.

"What do you mean?" Instead of running away, I'm intrigued. In retrospect, it's always my curiosity that drags me into trouble.

"I've got to report to a certain gentleman living in south Florida. Hmm, it looks like Nakamura hasn't told you about him and his kid, am I correct?"

"A gentleman in south Florida…? And his kid…?" I parrot like a total idiot. On my way to the 37th floor, I'd built my theory that the money Megu was paying to Dante was something related to the private project with Kakubeni, but things are looking a lot like blackmail, following his response. Then I recall the itinerary change of Megu's latest business travel to the U.S. Instead of staying there for another day in Texas, she came back earlier from Miami, on a private jet courtesy of her *client*. Actually, the whole office has been buzzing with this rumor that she met a beau in Florida… Wait a minute, he just mentioned a kid. Megu is in her early fifties. There were rumors that she'd divorced once, but no one has the guts to be nosy enough as to ask her about her previous marriage and kids.

"Earth to Sophie, are you there?" Dante calls me, looking down at me.

"I… I'm here…" I mutter, and then I blanche, realizing that I've lied that I'm her lesbian lover. What if he reports to his client about Megu being a pedophile lesbian? "Wait a minute! Dante, we have a serious misunderstanding. I mean, well… it's true that I've been living with Megu for a while, but that's only because she's such a nice and sweet person to take me under her wing. You know, Megu is a great person, and our relationship is just friendship, with business interests. She once helped me out when I was in trouble, and…" At this point, I'm practically clinging to him as I'm so desperate to convince him.

As I'm standing as tall as physically possible, looking into his bluish-green eyes, he's silent. And the next moment, he pulls away from me. Turning on his heels, he declares, "I'm gonna take a shower."

"Shower?"

"Wanna join me?" His tone is casual, but…

I can't run out of this suite without a proper explanation! Megu is my family, and I don't want the nasty rumors about her getting out. Wait a minute, Dante! We need to talk… Please…" I'm running after him as he heads for the bedroom.

The lights go on, probably working with a motion detecting sensor, illuminating the huge king-size bed and the color-coordinated furniture mainly in ivory and silver gray.

Without even glancing at me, he goes past the bed, unbuttoning his shirt. Wow, this suite's layout is identical to the one I've seen repeatedly in my dreams. The bathroom should be right around the corner.

On the way to the bathroom, he throws his

shirt onto the bed, exposing his tan, muscular upper body, prompting me to suck in air. I have teenage triplet brothers, but seriously, they're just a bunch of babies compared to him. Also, I've visited pools and beaches with my friends, but after all, most of them are musicians, and so far, I've never blurted out, "Why aren't you starring in some action movie?"

Oh my God... I've read about so many "armor of hard muscles" in books, but it's the first time ever for me to actually witness something living up to this expression. Overwhelmed by the provocativeness of his physique, I take a deep breath.

And the next thing I know, he comes back, walking towards me. I freeze, unable to process the sudden change of my status from being the huntress to the hunted.

"Hey, Sophie baby. I intend to be a gentleman, but when your guard is so low, as in how-low-can-you-go low, I must say that I'm tempted to take advantage of you." He lets out a deep sigh. "I happen to be heterosexual, and I'm younger than Nakamura by more than twenty years. Oh, by the way, never, ever mention you're open for a rape."

"Oh… sure… I didn't mean that. At that time, it seemed like a better option compared to broken bones and so on…" I mumble. "By the way, we need to talk, and I haven't checked your passport."

He rolls his eyes. "The passport's stashed in the bag sitting on the side of the bed. Go take a look. As soon as you're satisfied, leave here before I come out of the shower."

"But we haven't finished talking… Oh my God!" I jump about a foot as he starts unzipping his jeans right in front of me. Turning away from him so I don't see too much of his privacy, I'm sweating like a pig.

"If you're so desperate to make excuses for, whatever, you can wait for me in the bed. Of course, it's up to you. Rape isn't my cup of tea because most women throw themselves at me." As he talks, his voice sounds farther away, then I hear the noise of his jeans landing on the bed.

Ever so slightly, I move my head, hoping to steal a glance at him, but he's no longer in the bedroom. I let out a whoosh of air. Holy crap. I'm like a little rabbit wandering into the lion's den.

Wow, my dad and granddaddy were sooo right! They've always constantly argued about little things, but whenever they warned me about bad boys whom I shouldn't deal with, they always agreed with each other.

I let out a sigh, mulling over my thoughts. I'd been obsessed with him so much, seeing him in my dreams every night for a week now, only to face the cold, hard reality that he's completely out of my league. Who was I kidding? I should have never encountered him again. After all, I was happy when I didn't even know his name, admiring him like some sort of a rock star…

"Think priority, Sophie." I mutter to myself, shaking my head. Apparently, it's not the best moment for drowning myself in self-pity. Besides that, I'm here for my job. From what I've seen so far, Dante seems to be some sort of blackmailer, or something similar to that. In that case, isn't it risky for a member of a legitimate law firm, such as yours truly, to be involved with him? Something as trivial as receiving a very small gift—like a chocolate— might damage the reputations of Megu and her firm.

"Oh, yeah. This is so risky… Things could go even more south if he turns out to be some sort of mafioso…" I gasp. A cold and heavy feeling settling in the pit of my stomach.

Oh my God… What has gotten into me? After having gone through more than enough troubles in my life, my motto is supposed to be safety first, but… It's so true that life is so full of enigmas…

"Hey!" In the middle of my analysis, the bathroom door opens a bit, and Dante's head sticking out. "I'll be out of the shower in less than five minutes. So, make your decision fast and move faster. Or else..." With a snap of his fingers, the door shuts down.

"Or else?" I tilt my head, but no answer. I shrug, recalling how his tone was indifferent and uninterested. "Seriously, is it even possible to finish showering in five minutes?" It usually takes me about an hour to take a bath. Hey, the bathroom is a great place to relax—especially when the bathroom has only the bathtub and shower, without the toilet in the same room.

I close my eyes and take a deep breath. The

door to the bathroom is tightly shut, but somehow, I can hear the sound of water dripping… Is my imagination running in overdrive, or what?

Shaking my head, I walk toward the bed, and just like he's mentioned, there's a caramel-colored leather Boston bag sitting on the floor. The zipper has a lock, but right now, it's unlocked.

"Hello, let me check inside for the passport, okay?" I call to no one in particular. Call me chicken, but I'm not accustomed to ransacking a total stranger's bag without his presence.

Inside, most of the items are garments and nothing special. It looks like he travels light—on second thought, for someone staying here for at least a week, he's packed a little bit too lightly. When I travel overseas, I usually bring at least three suitcases—one small carry-on and two large ones—along with my violin. I need extra dresses and shoes for any last-minute changes. Of course, I also need the scores and care-items for the instruments, and yours truly.

"Maybe he's a good customer to the hotel's laundry service," I mutter to myself. "It's gross that he turns out to be one of those guys who are okay wearing the same garments for days. Still, he smells too good for such a slob…"

As I go on with my search while talking to myself, I finally find the passport in the zippered pocket of the bag. It's a U.S. passport, the same one I carry around the world. His name is Dante Kent Walker. I check for the stamps, but there are just a few of them. Assuming from his fluency in Japanese, I thought he was a frequent visitor here, but I was wrong. It was issued five years ago in Norfolk, Virginia.

"Oh… he's from the East Coast." Boston, Massachusetts, is written as the place of his birth. And he's thirty-four years old. "Mmm… he looks better in person. By the way, what if it's forged?" I raise the passport and inspect the hologram area.

The next moment, a shadow passes in front of my eyes, and… "Hey, are you implying that I'm visiting here on a forged passport?"

"Hyet!" I jump up, maybe about two feet. Honestly, he caught me by surprise. Given his track record of spooking me, I might be competing for the high-jump by the time I leave here.

"What does *hyet!* mean?" He cocks his head to the side, sitting on the sofa, clad in only a towel wrapped around his waist.

"Hyet means hyet! It's not really a word but some noise that pops out when you're spooked or surprised," I say. "By the way, that was a quick shower. Did you wash behind your ears?"

"What are you? A grandma?" He chuckles, but his dark blond hair has turned darker with moisture, and he smells even better with the scent of citrus-based fragrance. "I told you I'd be done in five minutes."

"Come on, go back and soak in the tub maybe? I'm sure they have lovely smelling bath salts."

"Oh, yeah?" He arched one of his eyebrows. "I was thinking about getting to know each other in bed, but doing it in the hot tub sounds like a plan."

"WHAT?"

"After all, you can't trust me, even after inspecting my passport." He shrugs nonchalantly.

"But, but, but… you said you don't… force

women to do… anything…" As I stutter, he sighs and steps onto the floor, by my side. "Wait a minute! I mean… stay!" I flip my hands in front of me, wishing that I could build a wall with that.

"I'm not domesticated, so I haven't learned to stay." He winks at me.

"Oh… Does that mean you're not married?" I mumble, and then I shake my head. "No, no, no… That's not the point. I... I have a question… about the check. What is that for…? Megu says this is personal, but making such a huge transaction in secrecy isn't normal, so… I mean, what's your relationship with her… if I may ask?"

"I can't give you many details, but the money is going to another guy. Basically, I'm just a middleman running an errand."

"The one in Miami? Is it something like child support?" Dante has suggested that Megu has a child there… Then again, I can't imagine Megu living separately from her child. Believe me, she's taken me, just a daughter of her acquaintance, under her wing, caring for me like her own daughter, so how can she live separately from her own child? Anyway, if she's keeping the child and the father of the child a secret, she must have good reasons.

"You're smarter than you look," he comments.

I'm tempted to shoot back, but on second thought, everything started with my lame and vain lie. Speaking of lies, didn't I go too far by pretending to be a lesbian partner of Megu? At first, I thought he was blackmailing my boss, so I got a little defensive, but assuming from the information I have so far, it seems like Dante is highly trusted by his client... What if he relays my lie to his client...?

"Look, I apologize for scrutinizing you. I know nothing about you, so I was confused." I lean toward him, hoping to show that I'm not his enemy. "And that's why I described my relationship with Megu... I mean, relationship might be a tricky word, but I must tell you there's nothing even remotely romantic between us. It's true we're living together for a while, but we've been sleeping separately the whole time. I cook, do laundry, and do some admin work for her in exchange for a good salary and living in the condo free of charge. As for the cleaning, Mr.

Roomba is mostly in charge, and we have once-a-week maid service." Trying my best to be convincing, I'm staring into his bluish-green eyes, completely forgetting about personal space and so on. "Also, I don't think Megu is a lesbian. Not that we've talked about sexuality, but... I don't think she's seeing anyone, and as far as I know, she hasn't been seeing anyone. And with full disclosure, I'm not a lesbian, I think. Not that there's anything wrong with that, but so far, I haven't felt the urge to chase hot women. Even the time when I met Sabrina Hahn, the virtuoso and the universe's hottest pianist, I didn't lust, and..."

Seriously, what am I talking about?

When our knees bump into each other, he touches my cheek, caressing down my neck. "Are you seducing me?" And the next thing I know, his large hand is holding the back of my head.

I open my lips, but I don't know what to say.

He clasps my right hand, which is still clutching his passport, and places it on his chest. Wow, I can feel his heart beating...

"I'm gonna touch you. If you want me to stop, just shove me away," he whispers into my ear in a tone so sweet and mesmerizing...

I can't say anything, and I don't have the guts to shove him...

Okay, I lied. Again. I don't want to shove him away.

On second thought, letting the emotions sweep me away is a bad idea, right? At least, that's what the voice of reason says... But the voice fades away as I'm captivated in his eyes. Oh my God... look at his face! He's sooo beautiful, as in heart-stopping. I'm so glad I'm not a sculptor. Otherwise, I'd be so jealous of whoever created him...

I close my eyes, mostly because they're growing dry as I'd been practically staring at him forever. One second after that, something warm and gentle presses on my lips, followed by something wet and hot parting my lips and coming in.

For a moment, my mind turns blank as if something sparkled with an extreme *bang!* complete with a thunderbolt, but then I realize that I'm choking. "Mmm... Melf... melf...Mahmomm... mneen!" I'm trying to say "Help, I can't breathe!" patting his arm, but I can't talk normally.

"You're supposed to breathe through your nose," he informs me, pulling away from me.

"Oh, okay. Thanks." I nod many times.

Dante grimaces, scratching his head. "Is this one of your tactics to imply the lack of romantic relationship with Nakamura?"

"Excuse me? Was that a test?" My eyes widen. Ooh... I'm so defiant! And, a little bit hurt. "Apparently, I've failed that unannounced test of yours." If only I could say something like, "It takes two to make a good kiss," looking cool and composed! Unfortunately, I'm panting like an old dog who'd just swallowed too much water while drowning.

"Are you all right? Take a deep breath... in... and out." He rubs my back, his touches deceptively gentle.

"Thanks... I feel better now..." I say, and I mean it. "By the way, do you offer retakes of the test?" I don't know what I'm thinking, but I'm standing on my toes so I can kiss him again.

"Absolutely." He leans in, and this time, we're really kissing. As in *kiss-till-you-drop* kind of kissing.

This time, I'm breathing through my nose while his tongue plays around in my mouth. Hmm… why do I feel heavenly good when I'm terribly lightheaded? I used to believe that connecting my mouth with someone else would be gross, and stewed or barbecued beef tongues are the only tongues allowed in my mouth, but I might have been wrong. Having his tongue in my mouth feels so… good, and I'm not even a cannibal.

"How was that this time?" I ask breathlessly as soon as our lips part.

"That was amazing." After a brief pause, he adds, "For a newbie student."

I roll my eyes. "Am I supposed to be honored?"

"Hell, I didn't mean to go this far." A smile appears at the corners of his lips. "I'm good at staying away from women with the slightest signs of complexity—mostly because I'm not thrilled about taking responsibility. I've never found fondness in innocent reactions… until now."

His smile reminds me of the chocolate he gave me when we met for the first time. "Do you happen to have chocolates? I mean, the ones you gave me outside the café?"

"The one I gave you was all I had unfortunately." A flicker of amusement crosses his eyes. "Why?"

"It tasted so good," I answer. "I went to the café, purchased a bagful of them, but none of them was even half as good as the one you gave me. What did you lace that one with?"

"I just unwrapped it and threw it into your mouth. Glad you loved it so much." With a low chuckle, he says, "Can I have something back as a thank-you token?"

Before I respond, the back zipper of my dress goes down with his nimble fingers. And the next thing I know, the dress slips down to my ankles. "What?" As I gasp, my shoulders are exposed, and I'm only wearing a chemise and bra—both black.

"I thought you'd be sporting something like white or pink." He whistles. "You never stop amusing me." His index finger runs across the cleavage between my breasts. Am I supposed to be clear and say I have two breasts? I've read somewhere that some women come with four or more breasts, so, just in case.

"You... you need to give me... more chocolates... to go further..." I manage to say, but of course, I have no idea about the definition of *further* in this context.

"That depends on the POV, I guess." His hand cups one of my breasts over my demi-cup bra. Kneading it softly like some kind of dough, he goes on. "Is it just me who feels like I'm the one entertaining you?"

"Um... I... I..." I think I have to object to him, but something is wrong. I mean... having his fingers on me feels... just good. I mean, good is the understatement of the year. Addictive is the more appropriate term.

"You're enjoying my company, aren't you?" he says knowingly. "With this pace, your name will come at the top of my lovers list."

I'm wondering whether to tell him about my addiction to his chocolate or him.

"Still, that option actually sounds good." His tone is not just seductive but sincere. "Hell, am I getting old, or what?"

"Um… Dante?" I manage to say, shocked at the sweetness in my whole body when I utter his name.

He holds me in his strong arms. "I had a feeling—or rather, something like a vision—when I caught you in my sight for the first time at that building. Back then, I thought I'd gone crazy because you looked too young for me."

"With full disclosure, I couldn't tear my eyes off you as I saw you coming out of the café… And I kept on seeing you in my dreams for… I mean… a week…"

He kisses my lips the moment I say those words. As his lips caress me, I close my eyes. I feel his fingers moving behind my back, and suddenly I can breathe more easily.

"Mm…" When I realize that my bra has been unhooked, and his palm is inside the cup of my bra, I shut my eyes even tighter. His hand feels so hot on my skin. As the kiss deepens, he starts caressing my hair. I might melt like butter in his suite…

Suddenly, my feet aren't touching the floor,

followed by the sound of something hard falling onto the floor. And the next moment, I fall onto my back into something so fluffy and creamy at the same time. I open my eyes a slit to find that I'm on the bed. My garments and shoes are scattered over the floor. Instead of tidying up the place, I'm watching every move of Dante's, thinking it'll be easier for him to undress himself. After all, all he has on is a bath towel.

Lying on my back, I'm watching his eyes. Goodness, it feels like I could watch his eyes forever and ever. His beautiful face comes close to mine, so I close my eyes again.

"Sophie, can you lift up your hip just a little bit?" he whispers, and his voice is so hypnotizing.

Without even clarifying, I do as he told me, and he undresses my lower body. Finally coming back to my senses, I gasp. "What? Oh, no. You can't look at me! I know how silly I look when only my lower body is dressed. It's like my upper body is sticking out of two boneless hams, and…"

"And looking very delicious." Chuckling, he undresses me completely, dodging my hands as I try to stop him.

"Come on. I don't have a runway-worthy body…"

"Look at your skin. It's so flawlessly smooth… just like the surface of a top-quality pearl." As he kisses the top of my breast, my toes curl.

"Oooh… did you close your… eyes…?" I moan as his tongue slides over my breasts, and then moves south. I'm so embarrassed that I want him to stop, but at the same time, I've never felt such powerful and delightful sensations in my life. I want him to continue.

"Rest assured, my eyes are wide open," he says casually. "Hey, can you call my name with your sweet voice? Oh, don't go using the last name, just in case."

"Dante…" His name rolls off my tongue as his fingers run down my stomach to the most private area of my body. It's been kept so private that I haven't even bothered with getting laser hair removal. After all, it was supposed to an area where nobody ever sees, so, just like that famous Schrodinger's cat being alive and dead at the same time, my pubic hair is here and not here at the same time.

"Hee!" I squawk as his finger touches the opening of… well… my vagina. "Wait a minute… That's not where you're supposed to touch… Oh, no… I've read many descriptions of finger-in-honey-pot situations, but I'm not quite sure if I'm ready to actually experience it myself…"

Babbling, I try to shut him off by closing my knees, but he blocks my attempt so easily. And the next moment, wet sounds echo in the bedroom.

"No need to worry. I won't make it painful, I promise." His whisper caresses my eardrums as his nimble finger brushes into me. As he has promised, I don't feel pain as his honey-grazed finger cuddles me. At least he's not lying, so far.

"Oh my…" I gasp as his finger brushes the sensitive flesh that I didn't even know existed in the first place.

"It's okay, Sophie. You're so beautiful…"

"Ya think…?"

"Absolutely." He kisses my ear. "Breathe slowly and relax… Oh, yes. You're doing great."

Oh, he rocks at motivating me, doesn't he?

"Sophie?" He calls my name abruptly. "What do you say about falling in love with each other? You and me, together?"

His low, husky voice booms in my ears. Oh my God... It's as if the much-desired sequel of the dream I'd seen for the past week has finally come out. Am I seeing an upgraded version of my erotic dream, or is everything happening here real?

After a while of mulling over my thoughts, my mind is set. Just let the sweet, sensual, and joyous wave sweep me away to wherever it takes me. If it turns out to be an upgraded version of my recurring dream, so be it. I'll cherish it like a treasure. After all, I have a hunch that I'll end my life as a virgin, so having something delicious, sexy, and delightful to hold onto for the rest of my life would be nice.

Even if it turns out to be a dream...

On second thought, I'm not giving much thought about the scenario if everything so far turns out to be real.

Chapter 4

Squeak…squawk…scratch! The out-of-tune noise produced with my Guarneri assaults everyone's eardrums in the lesson room #3 at a certain concert hall in Minami area in Osaka. I know it's far from music, but I can't remember how I used to play the violin. Under normal circumstances, I'd be saddened, frustrated, and devastated with another day with no sign of progress, but today, I'm too busy regurgitating a series of events that happened in the past two days.

What was I thinking? Questioning myself for the umpteenth time, I notice there's a bigger question in the picture. *What was he thinking? Why did he leave me like that? Without even proceeding to actual sex?*

Oh, yes. I'm obsessed with sex. Dad might have a heart attack if he learns his darling little angel has turned into a nymphomaniac.

I was in the bedroom of the suite where Dante was staying. He was mostly naked—sporting only a bath towel—and he was undressing me. My mind was set: I was ready to say goodbye to my virginity. But just then my purse fell to the floor, dumping its contents all over. I didn't really care, but Dante was nice enough to pick everything up. Why he stopped in the middle of his seduction is beyond me, but he did.

Unfortunately, my granddaddy's business card happened to be one of the items on the floor. He's a good guy, and it's fun to be around him, but he has this bad habit of sneaking his card into my purses. Having just his card might be fine as far as it's his professional card, but the ones he sneaks into my belongings have "Daniel Rowling, the COB of USCAB, Granddaddy of Sophie Rowling" written in bold letters. He used to be the CEO, and became COB—chair of the board—when he handed the company over to my dad.

"Oh, you're the granddaughter of USCAB's former CEO," Dante said, looking surprised.

My father's family has been running a relatively large security company for generations, and the Rowling men are rather famous among the people in security industries. Those people may or may not include groups like the mafia. But that's never discussed.

After finding out about my family, Dante was still sweet and seductive, but he didn't proceed to…what's the right word? Penetration?

What a shocker. I was so ready for my first-ever penetration, but apparently he changed his plan. I can only assume my grandfather's name had something to do with it. But looking back, if he was some shady blackmailer, going the whole nine yards would have had bigger pros than cons. I'm not sure how useful I'd be to a blackmailer, but according to the books I've read so far, bad guys tend to think they can use someone like me as some kind of a leverage. Maybe they would take me hostage or shoot a sex video, threatening my family to pay up or leak Sophie porn to the world. But I'm such a nympho that if my porn gets out on the internet, I'll download it and make some extra copies for keepsakes. If I had the pleasure of filming a sexy video featuring Dante and me, I'll have some kind of a souvenir to relive all the blissful moments, again and again…

Just saying!

That's only my wishful thinking. After all, he

limited himself to entertaining me with just the foreplay. He was so good that I passed out midway...I didn't even notice him leaving the suite. Don't get me wrong, I wasn't drugged or intoxicated. On the contrary, I was 100% sober, and I consented with him to proceed further... Imagine my shock when I learned that he'd checked out of the hotel, paying on my behalf for everything including new clothes, room service breakfast, and a special afternoon tea set from the gourmet shop, all for *his little sister*? I'm the first-born child and so far my parents have never mentioned anything about a big brother. Besides that, the way he entertained me in bed was far from something acceptable between siblings. Why did he make up such a blatant lie?

Two days following my unexpected encounter with Mr. Almost James Bond, a.k.a. Dante Walker, I'm practicing for an upcoming concert for Mrs. Ono's retirement. My music career might never be resuscitated, but at least I have great friends who are nice enough to do practice sessions with me. These same friends are also willing to play the concert as a quartet—in case my knack for playing the violin doesn't return by then. They say I should play with them as a quintet, but I'm skeptical. I have a feeling that I would be in the middle of the worst performance of my life.

Seriously, I'm a mess. A total mess. All because of what happened at the suite—or rather, what didn't happen there.

When I was three, Mr. Edelmann, the previous owner of my Guarneri and my first violin teacher, told me to focus on the violin and music whenever playing the instrument. He also taught me that a violinist's job is to help the instrument sing as beautiful as its destiny.

"Just relax and enjoy your partnership with Allegra. This is the most important part, you know." I can still hear his soothing voice in my ears. He passed away when I just turned twenty. He was hundred and eight years old. As much as I miss him, I feel blessed that he departed to a better world without witnessing my current situation.

Squeak, squawk... La, do, fa, la...

Wait a minute. Did I just produce some tolerable sounds?

"Sophie, what's happened to you?" Erika Miyata stops playing the piano and stands up.

"Did I just make some okay sounds?" I ask her. "Or was that something that happened only in my head?"

"You started crappy, but you produced la, do, fa, la so brilliantly!" Marie Sakamoto chimes in, looking around the room, adding, "Right? Right?"

"Yes, she did." Mike Fujiwara, the cellist, gives me a thumbs-up.

"Congrats, Sophie! You're recovering." Ken Takahashi, née Kato, the violist, applauds.

"Oh my God…" My jaw drops. "Can I try again?"

"Absolutely!"

La, si, do, re, mi, fa, sol, la… Do, sol, re, la, mi, si…

"Great job!" Marie jumps up. "Sophie, just trust yourself and have faith in you. I can almost hear you playing the first violin for the concert. You can do it!"

"You think so?" I tilt my head. "Actually, I was thinking you'd be the best fit for the first violin part in case I still can't play the instrument for the concert."

"No way! I'm in charge of the second violin," she says casually. "If you're not playing the first violin, what are you gonna do at the concert?"

"Dancing, perhaps?' Erika chuckles, prompting me to grimace. "Honestly, you guys should see Sophie's dance once in your life."

"No, you shouldn't." I shake my head. "I'm a terrible dancer."

"Don't worry, Sophie." Ken raises his hand. "You're a great violinist, so no one cares if you suck at dancing."

"That's right," Mike agrees. "So, what's happened? The last time, you were making noises like solfege has completely evaporated from you. I can already feel the virtuoso inside you waking up."

"Oh, no. No need to sugar coat your opinions." Flipping my hands in front of my face like crazy, I shake my head.

"Come on, we're musicians. Nobody says nice things to terrible noises just to be kind." Marie makes tsk-tsk sounds. "No offense, but your violin sounded pretty dead last week, but not only have you produced multiple sounds with the right tunes, the violin itself sounds alive. It may be still drowsy, but not dead anymore"

"Exactly!" Mike chimes in. "Actually, it was like looking at someone who got terribly injured in a train wreck trying to learn to walk again. I didn't have the heart to express my honest opinion because you sounded so… What's the right word? Um, well, you sounded so desperate and resigned at the same time. As much as you were desperate to play the music like the prodigy you used to be, but at the bottom of your heart, you'd already given up on the violin. It was like you were only waiting for someone, anyone to come and throw in a towel for you."

"That's right, Mike." Marie bobs her head again and again. "It's so true about cellists being highly observant."

"So true," Erika agrees and looks at me. "Of course, some details like articulation and trills need polishing, and you have to train yourself to actually play pieces of music. But I have a hunch you'll be playing the instrument like you used to. Perhaps, even more brilliantly, I guess. After all, it's not your body that hindered you from playing music. It was all about your heart."

"Oh… That's what my mom, professors, and doctors said." I chuckle. "I've heard about all the horror stories of a violinist playing tennis and mangling his arm, ending his career as a violinist forever. Hmm… I think I was really traumatized when I saw the shuttered Stradivarius, but in retrospect, I'm blessed that I'm physically unscathed."

As I mutter the last sentence, Marie widens her eyes. "Oh, I thought you were traumatized to see the dead body."

"Marie." Ken flips his arms and shushes her. "Let's not talk about it."

"Oh, it's okay." I shake my head. "Actually, when I woke up, the body had been already moved out of the suite, but I saw the splintered Stradivarius, and I was shocked."

"To see the broken violin?" Erika asks.

"Yes. The first thing I thought was 'WHAT? Has it been destroyed before I had a chance to try playing it?' I felt like I was so rejected by the instrument. After all, Stradivarius is… you know, special."

"So true." Mike nods. "The king of all the strings instruments."

"Come on, Stradivarius is so overrated." Erika shrugs. "Didja know Guarneri is waaay rarer, as the number of pieces still existing in the world is much smaller than Stradivarius?"

"Seriously?" Ken and I say in unison.

"I've read about it somewhere," Marie comments. "According to the article I came across, it's hard to tell which is superior to the other when both instruments are about the same in terms of historical importance, quality, and so on. One of the major differences is that Stradivarius is more widely known among the general population with little to no interest in strings music, and many rich people acquire Stradivarius as some kind of a commodity, instead of musical instruments. As for the instrument dealers, they're happy if they can earn more in commissions, and it's easier to do so by pushing Stradivarius more strongly than Guarneri. If I recall that right, there are approximately twelve hundred Stradivarius, compared to just two-hundred Guarneri pieces. You know what I mean?"

"Yes…" Nodding like a bobblehead, I mutter, "Oh my God… That bastard tricked me! He said that Stradivarius are the rarest violins in the world, and just touching it for once has a potential to make my music way more mature and sophisticated…"

"And, he did that terrible thing to you?" Erika snorted. "Honestly, I'm glad he's dead."

"Me, too. Good thing he didn't live long enough to actually rape me." I tilt my head, placing my violin into the carbon case and rolling my shoulders. "It's funny that my shoulders feel so light." Have I been carrying some invisible burden, or what?

"What? He didn't rape you?" Marie throws her arms up in the air. "Isn't that fabulous? Ooh… I thought you'd been… and, you're suffering from something like a PTSD."

"Come on, Marie. Stop rubbing salt in her healing wounds." Ken lowers his voice.

"Oops, sorry." She shakes her head. "Sometimes, I blurt out the most inappropriate things."

"It's okay, guys. No need for an apology." I chuckle. "I think we have a serious misunderstanding. It's true that I've been having trouble with the violin, unable to play the instrument like I used to, and it's a psychological problem. Then again, I'm not hurt about rape—because the rape never happened. As for the guy dropping dead, I sometimes remember him as a nuisance—as the person responsible for the nasty legal trouble in Paris, and absence of my BFFs. What traumatized me was the part that I stopped seeing and hearing Jackie and Allegra." I look around. "Jackie? Allegra? Are you there?"

No answer.

"Hello? Jackie? Allegra? Are you with us?" Marie calls out, and then looks at me. "Did they answer?"

"So far, I can't see or hear them yet." I shake my head.

"It's okay, Sophie. Even if you still can't see them, they exist, and if they're here with us here instead of with your mom, they would be delighted to see your recovery." Erika stands up, hugging me.

"Your mom says Jackie and Allegra are still looking after you. I believe her. I've never seen them personally, but sometimes, I can feel them. Remember how they gave me very helpful advice via you when we were in high school, practicing the instruments for college admission exams? They always cheered me up, and I'm forever grateful for them."

"They loved you, Erika. I think they still love you." I giggle, and I mean it.

"Wow, I wish I could see them, too," Ken says longingly.

"Now that you mention it, Jackie had a crush on you. She was like, 'Look at Ken! Isn't he hot? Hey, if I kiss him while I float around him, does it make me guilty of sexual harassment?' And, Allegra used to say 'As far as he doesn't notice you, it'll be okay. Besides that, the humans can't sue us the fairies and ghosts.'"

"Seriously?" Ken shifts, looking slightly uncomfortable.

"Aren't they hilarious?" Marie's hysterical laughter echoes in the room.

"The hottest violist, craved by the ghosts—Ken, you should seriously add this phrase to your slogan." Mike whistles. "But guys, don't share that episode with Ririko, okay?"

"Of course not. Jackie, are you with us? Ken here is married to wonderful, beautiful Ririko, and he's taken. So, you need to find a new crush." Erika wiggles her fingers.

"Come on, I don't know how to react when you put it like that. By the way, the episode of Jackie during our college days will just make Ririko laugh." Ken chuckles, turning to me. "Thanks for sharing the fun memories of Jackie and Allegra. So, are you feeling the signs of your ability to communicate with ghosts and fairies coming back?"

"Oh...?" I tilt my head, not quite grasping why he's asking that. Then I suck in air sharply. "Now that you mention it, I just recalled that I'd been fussing over them for more than a year. Actually, I'd been missing them so badly—way worse than I've missed playing the instrument. Of course, I still miss them, and I want to talk to them, but... With full disclosure, I haven't thought about them in the past two days… I still love them as my family, but I think I'd forgotten about them for a while."

"Hmm… you stopped thinking about them… because of what?" Marie leans in. "You don't look like you've got bigger worries. On the contrary, you look happy."

"Well…" I gnaw on my lower lip. "Technically, I'm more disappointed and confused than being happy. Um… I've been kinda… sorta… obsessed with something else?" Why do I sound like I'm asking a question instead of making a statement?

"Sophie, Sophie, Sophie." Erika's face turns serious. "We've got to discuss your obsession further. I have a feeling that your obsession is very good. After all, you've shown a significant improvement with your violin. Our time slot in this lesson room will be ending in five minutes. Let's pack our stuff up and move to Royal Century's tearoom. We'll make it in time for their teatime special."

"Yes, let's!" Mike is already moving his cello back inside the case.

"I can't wait to hear that." Marie is giggling like a kid opening Christmas presents.

"Oh, come on. Don't get your hopes too high. My story could be boring, you know," I say hurriedly.

"No worries, Sophie. Your stories never get boring." Ken winks.

* * *

"Oh my God! So, he was gone, baby, gone when you woke up the next morning?" Marie's jaw drops.

"Yes. Can you believe the shock of waking up with a phone call from the hotel's front desk? Informing me that my *older brother* has checked out? What was he thinking?" I munch on a spoonful of crème brulee, hoping to calm my fury with sugar and calories. This tearoom's crème brulee is great. Creamy, velvety, and crunchy at the same time.

"Hmm, he was seductive at first, but he didn't go the whole nine yards." Erika raises an eyebrow and turns to Ken and Mike. "Guys, how do you interpret this situation?"

"That's a good question." Ken tilts his head uncomfortably.

"Are you sure he wasn't some sort of a

creation of your imagination?" Mike asks, adding, "Just saying!" as I narrow my eyes at him.

"Here's exhibit number one to prove his existence." I take out the check I was supposed to drop at Phoenix International's front desk. "See? Here's the sender's name, Megumi Nakamura, signed here, right? This here is the name of the recipient. And, you see the red letters overlapping the signature?"

"Oh, okay. It looks legit," Mike comments, inspecting the check.

"Right." Marie nods, taking a bite of her pistachio ice cream. "Does it say 'See you later'?"

"Yes. Actually, it's the most confusing part." I let out a sigh. "So, he's gone, leaving me all alone in the hotel's suite. It looks like I'd been dumped, right? Then again, he was too—what's the right word? Gentle, maybe?—for someone who abandoned me. First off, he had the meal and brand-new clothes all arranged and delivered to me in the morning. And, he went so far as to prepare a box of afternoon tea set from the gourmet shop, *after* paying for everything. Also, he'd paid for the limo service to the condo, and the chauffer had to ask the condo's concierge guy to sign a delivery strip. If he were some kind of a fraud, he'd have just left me there, without paying for anything at all."

"That's a good point," Erika agrees. "So far, he sounds more romantic than criminal to me. Like, he really cares about you."

"And, he must be rich," Mike interjects. "He's either rich, an idiot, or both. Otherwise, who'd doodle on the check worth three hundred grand, ruining it?"

"And, that hotel is really pricey. If I recall that right, the average room charge for the presidential suite at Phoenix International is over five thousand USD per a night. Ririko was talking about staying there for a romantic weekend. Hey, Sophie, how was the suite? Did it live up to the cost?"

"I suppose so. The bedroom and living room were stylish, and the bathroom was so… heavenly." I smile, recalling the short but memorable stay at the hotel. "As for the bathroom, I was already alone when I visited there, but I liked their jet bath. Also, the toilet was in a separate room, which earned extra points in my heart."

"Of course, the toilet has to stay away from the bath and shower," Erika agrees strongly. "I don't know why they put the toilet in the same room as the bath facilities at most western hotels. Don't they feel like they're taking a bath, surrounded by toilet cooties?"

"Oh, yeah. What if you poop just before taking a shower?" Marie makes gagging sounds. "So icky."

"Even worse, what if the poop happens to be diarrhea?" Mike cracks out laughing. "Gross. That's why I hate visiting my dad's side of family in Canada. No matter how much I love them, I hate taking a bath in the same room as the toilet bowl. I need a solid wall between the bath and the toilet."

"Why are we having such a heated discussion on the bathroom?" I'm giggling. "By the way, Ken, the hotel's food was great. Their breakfast omelet was to die for, and they offered a great selection of bread. Oh, and the sausages were delicious."

"Fabulous. I'll share that info with Ririko." He nods happily.

"You're a damn lucky guy, Ken. You're like a

man version of Cinderella," Mike teases. "I mean, in a very good way."

"Swoon!" Marie makes kissy noises. "Ririko fell in love with you when she saw you playing the viola at a concert for her company."

"And we were still college students," Erika chimes in.

"Yeah. Ever since she discovered Ken, I've been making sure that I look and perform my best at any concerts—especially concerts at offices, but so far, no Queen Charming has found me." Mike shakes his head.

"What a shame." I make sympathetic noises, smiling. "But the best is yet to come."

"Where's my Prince Charming? Where's my Prince Charming? Where's my Prince Charming?" Erika says in a sing-song tone.

"You're repeating it three times because it's very important, right?" Marie chimes in.

"Absolutely. Now that Sophie has found her Prince Charming, it's about time I find mine."

"Um… Erika, I'm not sure if Dante's my Prince Charming…" I tilt my head. I've already nicknamed him Mr. Almost James Bond/Mr. Danger/Mr. Wrong, and he ditched me at the hotel.

"I don't know about the Royal Charming things, but regardless of his identity, I can tell Dante is someone very special for you." Ken's tone is more confident than ever.

"Oh…?" I look at him, trying to read between the lines.

"He's special, you know. The time you spent with him was huge enough to kick everything else out of your mind," he continues.

"I guess you're right." I nod. "I forgot to think of Jackie and Allegra for the first time since I've lost my perception on them."

"What matters the most is that your music is coming back from a long vacation, you know." Ken chuckles. "Resuscitating your dying music—or rather, the music you're in the middle of murdering—is a truly hard job to do, and it's not something a random stranger walking into your life can do. Whoever does that is very *very* special for you."

"I can imagine." Erika nods.

"Thanks." Ken continued, "When I was in my

senior year at college, I was considering quitting the viola for good."

"Seriously?" Mike widens his eyes.

"Yes. I'd been getting way too many rejection letters from the orchestras I'd applied to. It felt like I was going nowhere. So, I started interviews for positions completely unrelated to the viola, and actually, the reason I went to Takahashi Holdings for the concert was just because I wanted to check out the company prior to taking an interview for a position of administrative assistant. Back then, I was so young that I thought mentioning something like 'I've been to this building lately. I was playing the viola, as a member of Kyoto Music College's chamber orchestra,' would help me get a job with them." Ken chuckles. "In retrospect, my plan would have just confused the interviewer. But luckily, Ririko discovered me, became my sponsor, and urged me to pursue the viola no matter what."

"Mmm… how sweet is that?" Marie mutters dreamily.

"Actually, not quite so, at first." Ken shakes his head. "Like I said, I was young and childish back then, and I said something like 'Thanks for the generous offer, but I'd like to pursue something more realistic and stable.'"

"Come on, man. Were you an idiot, or what?" Mike throws his hands in the air.

"Yes, I was. But, at that time, I was sort of obsessed about quitting the viola. Maybe I was tired, or maybe I got bored, but back then, it felt like there was this wide world waiting for me outside the prison of the viola. When I announced my plan to my parents, I was afraid of their fury—especially, my mom's—but instead of going berserk, she was quietly sobbing while my dad was sighing nonstop. So, now that my mind was set, I was determined to get a real job. Then, in came Ririko's offer. Of course, I knew there were musicians who'd kill to have Ririko Takahashi sponsor them, but I was such an asshole to think like, 'Hell, I don't want to be appear like some manwhore... her little pet. So, what'll happen when she gets bored with me? Right now, I'm still young enough to pursue other careers, but if I waste some more years with no experience as an office worker? I'll be just an older guy with no other skills but playing the viola. No thanks!' Just like that."

"Ken, you were such an idiot." Mike grimaces. "We're talking about Ririko Takahashi, the heiress and the vice president of Takahashi Holdings, one of the biggest general contractors in Japan, and you said no to her offer?"

"Yep, an idiotic asshole," Erika comments. "Not only that, she's hot as hell."

"What's wrong with being a manwhore? If I were you, I'd have thrown myself at her, fucking her so hard that she can't forget me—ever," Marie says matter-of-factly as we fall into an awkward silence. "Hey, why are you guys being so quiet? Did I say anything weird?"

Ken clears his throat. "Anyway, she practically kidnapped me so I couldn't run away from the youth chamber orchestra to perform at the Embassy of Japan in Berlin. She was so thorough, assigning the security guards to haul me onto the plane, and their mission was all about detaining me instead of protecting me."

"Wow, that's extreme." Erika widens her eyes.

Marie giggles. "Good thing we musicians tend to have higher threshold for threats. Otherwise, you could have died from shock."

"I know!" Mike and I say in unison.

"When I was little, my mom used to punch one of those electric pianos, trying to knock absolute pitch in my then little body." Mike shakes his head. "When I was slow to answer, her hand used to fly over my cheeks, for the crime of irritating her with my slow answer."

"Nowadays, most of our parents could be in jail, accused of child abuse," Erika comments.

"But back then, moms attempting to push their kids into college for music had to take extra-tough stances on their kids. After all, what kind of eight-year-old kids practice some instrument for six to ten hours a day, without incentives?" Marie rolls her eyes. "In my childhood, things like my mom getting mad for me not practicing enough, putting my violin in a garbage bag, leaving it at the dump site, and little *moi* running after her, retrieving the violin, sobbing, practically happened five hundred times a year. And, whenever I return home from the dump site, the door is locked. What kind of a mother was she?"

"That didn't happen to me. The piano was too heavy to carry to the dump site." Erika wiggles her fingers. "But when I lied about finishing my piano practice for the day, my mom pinched my lips with her iron claws, yelling, 'Is this the mouth that keeps on lying?' I was so scared that I bled from my nose."

"So hilarious!" I giggle. "When I was lazy on my practice, my mom sent Allegra and Jackie to me, and the fairy-ghost duo kept on bitching till I came back to practicing. Unlike physical noises, you can't get away from their nonstop chattering with earplugs and so on. One time, I ignored them for an hour or so and Jackie sang Queen of the Night aria nonstop until I went back to practice. And, I was sobbing." As I say, I notice that I'm not sobbing as I talk about my paranormal BFFs ever since I've lost my perception on them.

"*Fühlt nicht durch dich! Sarastro Todesschmerzen! Sarastro Todesschmerzen!*" Marie sings the part about the toxic mom demanding Sarastro punish her own daughter with pains of death. She giggles, still singing "I'm sooo terrible. I'm no expert of coloratura."

"Bravo!" Mike hoots and we all applaud.

"Thanks for a very memorable performance, Marie. And thank you guys, for sharing all the interesting stories. After your story, the part about my getting kidnapped and detained sounds like nothing." Ken chuckles. "Still, this opportunity in Berlin changed my life forever. After having the pleasure of performing under the mentorship of very amazing Professor Thomas, I went to Vienna as a tourist, and honestly, Vienna Philharmonic Orchestra's performances at the golden Musikverein were so mind-blowing. For the first time in my life, I sobbed like a drunken idiot in the concert hall. I was like, 'Holy shit, I've practically accomplished nothing with my viola, and am I quitting now? Hell no. Gotta keep on my life with the viola no matter what.' Seriously, it was like all the energy and motivation came back all at once. Before that moment, I thought I'd completely lost my passion in music. In retrospect, before visiting Berlin and Vienna, I used to play the viola for my own sake. But while I was still in Vienna, I was itching to play the instrument in front of Ririko. Honestly, it was the first time I truly longed to play the viola in front of someone in particular, I mean, someone special."

"Isn't that fabulous?" I say, and I mean it.

"Yup. As soon as I came back to Japan, I went to see Ririko to thank her for everything, and to beg her to listen to my viola. After my performance, she said, 'Keep on playing the viola. I don't know how many people would like your music, but at least, I love it, and I want to listen to your viola for the rest of my life. So, keep playing the instrument till I die. Don't forget that longevity runs in my family, so, be prepared for a very long, never-ending career.' I didn't care about what others would say anymore. Anyway, it's really powerful to have someone special—even if just one person in the world—you want to play your music for. I'm still determined to play the viola for the rest of my life. Hopefully, she'll love listening to my music, but even if she gets sick of it sometime in the future, I'll still have the memory of her loving my viola."

"Lucky you. I'm impressed," Mike says.

"So true. It's so amazing to have someone you

want to play your music for…" With a contented sigh, Marie turns to me. "In your case, Dante is definitely your special person. After spending less than one night with him, you've managed to produce appropriate pitch. You've got to think of him when you touch the violin, okay? I have a hunch your virtuoso playing style will be back soon by trying to play the instrument for his sake."

She has a point. I nod. "Okay. I'll try." Then a sigh slips out of me. "Still, he may not like me. At first, he seemed so willing to go the whole nine yards, but he stopped with just kisses and foreplay. Perhaps, he found me too much of an amateur… Or was he avoiding me? Because I'm not skilled at kissing and so on? I got almost choked to death during my first kiss with him because I didn't know how to breathe. Is that the reason he checked out of the hotel before I woke up?"

"Those are tricky questions. I have no idea about your skills with kissing because we've never kissed before." Erika knits her eyebrows. "Maybe it's best if you ask Dante yourself?"

"But, how?" I say grudgingly. "He didn't even

bother to give me his number, email address, or social media account."

"But he's left this message here, saying 'See you later,'" Mike points out. "Maybe he's like 'I'll give you a ring when the right time comes' type of a guy?"

"Why do you sounding like you're asking a question?" I roll my eyes.

"How about asking Megu for his info?" Marie tilts her head. "After all, she's the one dealing with Dante, so she must have a lot more info than you already have. Speaking of Megu, how did you explain your impromptu hotel stay to her? It sounds like you ladies are really close, right?"

"We're very close, but right now, she's on another trip. Actually, she left for the U.S. just hours after sending me to Phoenix International." I let out a sigh. "I learned about her travel by listening to the message she'd left on her landline phone. The previous night, I didn't even send her a text message, informing her that I wasn't coming home."

"You missed each other. Ooh, what a relief…" Marie lets out a whoosh of air.

"That's exactly what I thought," I agree with her. "Her absence is one of the reasons I have more time for the violin. But I hope she comes home soon. I tried to reach her but so far, we haven't talked to each other. I hate time difference."

"Me, too. Time difference is a bitch." Mike nods.

"If it were a book or movie instead of my life, he'd pop up in front of me like a capricious ghost…" I shake my head, reaching for my teacup.

"Here's one thing I'm certain of," Ken interjects. "When things work out brilliantly, everything will be perfect no matter what. I don't know how to put it, but that's how things are designed, you know."

"Oh, yes. As we hang out here, munching on cakes and drinking tea, he might just come across with you, Sophie." Erika winks at me.

"Hmm… I'll keep my eyes wide open." I shrug, moving my gaze from our table to the lobby, and… "It can't be…"

"What's up?" Marie looks at me questioningly, but I can't give her an immediate answer.

A tall, muscular figure is crossing the lobby. I can only see him from the back, but he's so much taller—at least a head taller—than others coming and going, and I've seen that dark blond hair before. Today, he's dressed in a dark suit. As I follow him with my eyes, he goes out of the hotel's entrance.

"I may have just spotted him." Putting enough money to cover everybody's charges on the table, I stand up and clutch my stuffs. "I'll check out if it's him. Thank you all, guys. See you later!"

"Good luck!"

"Ciao!"

Waving to my friends as they encourage me from behind, I start running.

Chapter 5

Outside of the hotel, it's already dark and the sun has been replaced with the neon signs in the busy section of the town full of bars, restaurants, and pachinko gambling parlors—and it's not working on my behalf.

With the colorful lights sparkling, it's hard to tell the difference between Dante's dark blond and others with bleached and dyed hair. To make it worse, it's Friday night, and the town is practically packed with people ready to have fun.

But at least I have an advantage; he's very tall.

As soon as I start looking for someone taller than others by at least a head, I mutter, "Gotcha." Once I've located him, catching up with him should be easy as pie, right? Oh my God, am I a genius, or what?

Of course, things don't go as smoothly as I wish. I can see Dante but can't get close enough to talk to him, with a horde of people clogging the street. And the difference of our height—mostly, the length of the legs—isn't nice to me.

Calling his name isn't much of an option with all the venues on both sides of the road practically blasting loud music. So, basically, it's more like I'm staking him out than catching up. On second thought, maybe following him to the new place he's staying is a better option.

Wowza! I love my new plan, and it's getting so much fun.

As we move away from the train station, the crowd is getting slightly smaller. Keeping a steady distance, my eyes are focused on the back of his head. Maybe I'm good at doing this private investigator-ish thing. After all, my father's side of the family has worked for the FBI for three generations, and my mom used to be the feds' star investigator when it came to cases involving ghosts.

Clutching the carbon violin case protecting my Guarneri, I follow him. Seriously, he looks hot as hell, dressed in a charcoal gray, classic fit suit. His attire du jour somehow reminds me of the gentlemen working for the bodyguard section of USCAB. Maybe because of his physique and the cut of the suit coming in American Classic, as frequented among USCAB people including my dad?

"Oops, I'm so… sorry…?" I apologize as my purse bumps a total stranger, but as my eyes register, I trail off sounding more like a question. The guy I banged into looks super-busy, in the middle of a lip-lock with a lady. Hating to disturb them having fun, I step aside, quietly.

Wow, I wasn't paying much attention to my surroundings, but right now, I'm walking in an area mostly consisted of love hotels. A love hotel is typically a hotel where couples visit to have fun and have sex. According to what I've read and heard so far, a typical love hotel has a huge Jacuzzi complete with colorful, blinking lights, a huge bed that moves like a turntable, and a swing. Unfortunately, I haven't yet visited any love hotels, as they don't accept solo customers.

Speaking of being solo, at this point, I'm the only person walking alone in the neighborhood, and some of the couples around me are glancing at me with apparent suspicion. Okay, it's time to go back to my mission and catch up with Dante.

Wait a minute. Where is he? I look around, but he's nowhere in my sight. Still, he was heading forward the last time I checked, so I hurry along my way.

And the next thing I know, I'm wandering in an alley, and it doesn't look nice. Unlike the busy streets, it's way darker with less lights. It's littered here, smelling shady, and I see dubious-looking people here and there.

As it's dark, I move my gaze to the ground—mostly because I don't want to step on nasty things and fall. Oh my God… it's getting scary…

As I look around, my eyes meet with those belonging to a Latino-looking guy coming in my direction. When I notice that the loud patterns of his sleeves are tattoos instead of fabric, I look the other way. Basically, people showing off their tattoos in public is bad news. They're either lowlife scum, antisocial psycho criminals, or both. Good thing he looks busy as he's talking on the phone.

Desperate to return to the safer environment, I power walk. Good thing I can see the broader and busier street, complete with the vehicle traffic and decently dressed people walking around.

With a small sigh of relief, I slow down a little bit. "Whew… That was quite an adventure." Muttering to myself, I can only think of going back to my current home, sweet home.

As I keep on walking, the sound of a car engine approaches me from behind. Honestly, bad areas must have reasons to be shady—such as the locals lacking common sense. Driving on such a narrow path is dangerous and crazy. I step aside to the edge of the alley, just to avoid getting run over by this shabby van.

I frown as the bumpy Honda comes closer. Honestly, I've never seen such a scruffy car in Japan. With so many dents on the body and the paint peeling off, this vehicle can't pass the mandatory vehicle inspection tests!

But the bigger problem is now that this van stops right in front of me, like it's blocking my way. And, before I move away from this rotting chunk of garbage, the back side door slides open, three apparently non-Japanese guys come out, scoop me up, and then haul me into the rusting vehicle.

The next moment, I'm lying on the van's floor, clutching the violin case with my arms. Unlike the Toyota vans popular among people of all ages here, the third-row seat has been removed. I'm not sure if it's good or bad, at least I'm still in one piece, and nothing, including my Guarneri and myself, seems to be damaged.

The men in the van are talking in what sounds like Spanish. Then again, it could be Tagalog, or Vietnamese. Heck, I speak Japanese and English, along with a little German, French, and Italian, but the rest of the languages are pretty much gibberish to me.

"Hello? What's going on?" I ask, but nobody answers, and the door that swallowed me shuts.

Ooh-oh, it doesn't look good.

Then the passenger door opens, and the Latino-looking guy that I previously avoided gets in. He needs to improve his manners as he doesn't even say hi to me.

In the van, there are a total of five men— probably in their twenties to thirties—and they don't look so friendly. The passenger door closes and the car starts moving.

Oh my God… What's gonna happen next? Are they mugging me? I knit my eyebrows. Today, I'm not wearing jewelry pieces, and they haven't demanded my purse yet. Then again, that doesn't mean they're not evil muggers.

I tighten my grip on my violin case containing my precious Guarneri. If I recall, my granddaddy paid something more than 2 million dollars to purchase this piece. If you include the lessons, mentoring fees, travel and accommodation costs for Mr. Edelmann, the total cost should be more than 4 million. According to Marie, the market for historical instruments is pretty heated nowadays, so basically, my violin can fetch 5 million or more at auction.

On second thought, none of them look like a classical music aficionado. Rap or hip-hop fans, maybe? In my opinion, they look like the villains from the *Fast & Furious* series, and… Oh my God, now I want to puke. I've only watched the trailers, but if I recall that right, the villains of the movie franchise seemed to have no remorse over stealing, raping, killing, and committing all kinds of evil... Right?

Suddenly, I want to go home and take a nice soak in the extra-spacious bathtub at Megu's condo. At least, get the hell out of this crappy van. Wishing they'd change their plan and let me go, I stare at them, but they're busy talking. On the plus side, they haven't snatched my violin yet. Still, they could be discussing their plan to kill me, dismember me, and dump my body parts at multiple sites—after stealing my Guarneri.

As I imagine my tragic future, I feel so grim. I'm so disappointed in myself, and I feel so sorry for my family and all the shareholders of USCAB. It doesn't take rocket science to assume the stock price of a security company will plummet when the CEO's daughter ends up kidnapped and brutally murdered.

The saddest part is that I'd be saying goodbye to this world before recovering my ability to talk to Allegra the fairy and Jackie the ghost. Add that I'll be raped by those dirty gorillas before getting murdered!

"Why didn't you go the whole nine yards, Dante?" I mutter, shaking with anger, frustration, and resentment all rolled into one. Honestly, I was attracted to him, and I wanted to make love with him.

It was supposed to be my very first time having sex, after all. Am I asking too much, wishing to do it with someone I actually like? Besides that, it could have been not only my first but last as well...

The vehicle starts to speed up in spite of its bad shape. Oh, yeah, it's like a miracle. What a shame... If only they'd chosen something else as their mode of transportation—say, like, VW, or Renault—the car should have already stopped moving as it'd be busy coughing and spitting phlegm like a terminally ill lung cancer patient. Why should they use made in Japan cars just because they're in Japan? Come on, Honda! You guys should stop making good cars so that the car manufacturers in the rest of the world can actually compete with y'all!

And the next thing I know, the car shakes with a tremendous shock—like a meteor has hit the roof.

"What the...?" I blurt out as I notice the roof of the van is badly dented. Good thing I was already lying on the floor.

As I tighten my hold on the violin case, the vehicle is shaking like mad, and the gorillas are now shrieking and screaming in apparent panic. I'm so clueless, but at the same time, it's nice to see the gorillas freaking out. After all, I don't like their attitudes, and I really hate their ugly tattoos.

Exactly seven seconds later following the initial shock, a loud scream comes from the front seat. The driver hits the brake, prompting the car to jump.

Pursing my lips so that I don't bite my tongue, I look at the driver's seat. The front glass looks white with countless cracks a la a spider web. Apparently, this car can't drive anymore unless they replace the front glass pronto.

One of the gorillas opens the sliding door, and once the first one gets out of the car, others follow him like a horde of lemmings, apparently cussing in their language. The one closest to me grabbed my skirt, prompting me to gasp. At this point, I can't do anything but to brace myself to be raped and brutally murdered—especially when he takes a butterfly knife out of his pants pocket and flashes it in front of me.

But instead of slashing me and drinking my blood, he yells something in gorilla language. I'm not a primatologist, and I have no idea what he's talking about, but I nod like a bobblehead. Luckily, he's satisfied with my response. Still gripping the knife in his hand, he gets out of the van.

Under normal circumstances, I'd be pumping my fists, screaming something in the lines of "Yeahhhhh!" but I'm still quiet—mostly because I'm not yet alone, with the driver still remaining in the front row.

If only I were carrying a tranquilizer gun disguised as a watch! I bite my lower lip. If I were carrying one of those gizmos like Conan Edogawa, the detective from *Case Closed* series, the driver would be asleep by now. Maybe it'd be best that I talk to my dad or granddaddy to develop one of them— well, if I manage to survive tonight.

As I'm mulling over my thoughts, praying the driver falls asleep, he lets out a low groan, and the vehicle's engine stops.

"What?" My eyes widen. Did I just do it with my will power? Have I acquired a new ability to sort of force-stop things and people? Like, cutting off the power grid or something like that?

So many questions are literally flying across my mind, but then I notice I have something waaay more urgent to take care of, such as getting the hell out of here.

To my delight, the sliding door is ajar, and thanks to the old model of the car, it's not one of those auto-closure types that come with Toyota minivans. If I'm lucky, I might be able to get out of here. I look around me, making sure that I'm carrying all of my belongings, and I start moving. Little by little, praying for the best—

Bang!

"Hyet!" I shriek as the sliding door opens up in full.

"Sophie! Are you all right?" Before I pretend that I can't even imagine sneaking away, Dante calls my name, sticking his upper body inside the vehicle.

"Wh-wha…what?" I stutter. I have so many questions, but I don't know where to begin. Okay, so considering that I'm here, following Dante, so, in a way, I've achieved my goal to find him. Except, I lost track of him on the way. How did he find me? And, what about the gorillas that kidnapped me?

"Are you hurt?" he asks.

"I… I… I don't think… so…"

"Good." He leans on the door, reaching for his tie and starts loosening it up. "You scared the hell out of me."

Did I just make it through this situation all fudged up? I wonder. Maybe it'd be better if I stand up and leave here, but somehow, my legs aren't cooperating with me. There are many questions ranging from what happened to the van's roof to how the goons vanished, but at this moment, only the part that Dante has come to my rescue seems to matter.

"Come on, baby." He scoops me up with one arm, and I don't mind him calling me baby. I'm still shaky, but nothing hurts, and I can walk by clinging to him.

When I come out of the vehicle, we're still in the narrow alley, but we're quite close to the main road. The most notable part is that a total of six gorillas haven't left the scene—mostly because they're all on the ground, groaning and moaning, and apparently in physical distress.

"Um… did you… do that to them?" I look up at him, not quite sure how to react.

"They wanted to play with me, so I went

along." He shrugs nonchalantly.

"But…" I gasp as one of the gorillas stop moving. "Oh my God… I think he's dead."

"Come on, he's alive. I didn't hit him so hard." He lets out a chuckle. "Then again, don't you think kidnappers and rapists deserve to die?"

"But I don't want you to get arrested or hurt. You can never tell what those animals are up to," I say, still clinging to him. My voice is shaking.

"Rest assured, staying out of trouble in Japan is my motto. Still, if these goons are stupid enough to attempt to harm you again, then I'd have to kill them all."

As his hold on my hip tightens, my eyes widen and my heart jumps. He didn't sound like he was kidding when he mentioned the killing part as casually as grocery shopping, and as much as it frightens the heck out of me, I feel fuzzy in the stomach at the same time—like, I've become someone special for him.

Wait a minute! I'm tempted to bury my face in his broad chest, I need explanations from him regarding why he didn't finish having sex with me. I also need his explanation for leaving me in the suite while I was asleep. On top of all, I've got to tell him that I love him, and ask him out. It could be just me, but I feel some kind of chemistry between us.

Before I open the conversation, Dante moves, and he's fast. Pushing me behind his back, he yells, "Yo motherfucker! Are you fucking running away, leaving your friends?"

I take a peek and see the driver scurrying away, and when he looks back, I see blood on his face. The driver shouts something in a language I don't understand, but it must be bad—as Dante clicks his tongue and shoots back.

"What language was that gorilla talking?"

"Honduran Spanish with a touch of gorilla," he replies. "Did I just offend the gorilla community?"

"Hmm, so, they're Hondurans. I've never seen Hondurans before…" I tilt my head. Where the heck is Honduras? Then I realize they could be some kind of a mob newly invading Japan. Assuming from what they've done to me, I come across with this hypothesis that they could be after valuable instruments. In the music community in Japan, instruments worth millions of dollars are pretty common. Not to mention that most students majoring music in Japan have more expensive instruments than those owned by professional orchestra members in the West. "I'm gonna call the cops. I want them behind the bars before others get mugged and so on…"

Trying my best to put on a tough façade, I take a few steps from him. I want to congratulate myself for keeping my purse in my death grip, along with the violin case. Taking my phone out, I'm ready to—

"Wait a minute, calling the cops won't be a— Sophie, watch your back!"

"Wha—?" I look back, and a dark face jumps in my sight, scaring the bejeezus out of me. It's the guy who grabbed me and dragged me into the van. To make it worse, he's holding the butterfly knife, with the blade aiming at my neck. Instead of running away or jumping up and kicking the goon in the head, I'm frozen like a total idiot, watching the silver blade approaching me.

And the next thing I know, Dante holds me in

one arm, and the knife blade slashes his suit sleeve. And probably his forearm…

"Dante!" I shriek his name, looking up at him.

His face is unreadable, but I can feel him holding his breath.

The guy with the knife stops moving. He's putting his weight on the knife, but it won't go further in. So he attempts to pull it out, but the knife doesn't even budge.

Then it's Dante's turn to move. He smashes his elbow on the apparently panicky Honduran's face, knocking him out cold. And I'm talking about the arm with the knife sticking out of it…

My jaw drops.

"The son of a bitch…" Cussing under the breath, he shrugs. He yanks the blade out of his arm and tosses it on the ground. "Instead of appreciating my courtesy, this bastard ruins my best jacket. What's the world coming to?"

Despite the situation, the way he says those words makes me chuckle.

The police siren echoes from somewhere.

"Oh, someone called the cops…" I let out a

whoosh of air.

"The cops? I don't wanna waste my time with them. Let's go."

For a moment, I stop walking. I'm the victim of an attempted kidnapping and mugging, and Dante's the hero who rescued me out of the mess. Does that mean he's also some kind of a criminal...? According to the documentary shows featuring the cops, those who want to do nothing with the police tend to come from the shady side of the society. The problem is if it'd be a good idea to hang around with such a person. As a child of USCAB's CEO, I have some compliance to follow and so on...

"Suppose the authorities find out that I've been involved in an act of violence, I could face an immediate expulsion from this country. In that case, it'll be goodbye for us. Sophie, can you give me some time to spend with you?" He looks into my eyes, prompting my heart to skip a beat.

Oh, yes. I don't want him to go, so let's ditch the option with the police.

I suck in air as I see a streak of red blood running down his right hand, dropping to the ground.

"We need to visit the ER." The moment I say, he looks at me like that was the stupidest thing he's ever heard. I clear my throat, adding, "If you're not seeing the doctor, I'll treat your injury."

"Sounds like a plan." He winks at me, then takes my hand with his good hand. "Let's go."

Leaving the goons lying on the ground, we leave the scene.

Chapter 6

Here are the things about Dante Walker. He's crazy, smokin' hot, and *crazy*.

Okay, I mentioned crazy twice, but sometimes, you need repetition for emphasis.

"Sophie, why don't you chill a little and breathe slower?" His tone is lighthearted as we walk away from the totaled Honda van. "Putting a smile on your face will also help."

"You're asking too much," I say through gritted teeth.

If only my legs weren't shaky now, I'd be running like hell while screaming like a banshee. Aside from my wobbly body, what's keeping me from rushing in panic is Dante's adamancy for keeping calm—to avoid getting unwanted attention.

"Come on. Life is short. You've got to have fun while you can." His tone is teasing.

"That's like asking for a pig to fly." I roll my eyes.

"I wouldn't mind seeing a pig, cow, or

elephant fly. We'll have a little chill time over there."
With his good arm wrapped around my waist, he
leads me to a small park. As we walk past the cutesy
promenade romantically lit up, I'm sure we're
blending in with other couples hanging there, chilling
out.

"Imagine a day that's mostly sunny with a
chance of raining cattle. It won't be pretty," I point
out.

"Relax. Let's have a seat." He steers me to an
unoccupied bench in a shadowy area. "Hey, do you
happen to be carrying some tampons? Or maxi pads?"

"Maxi pads?" I look up at him in a shock.
"Are you having a period?" I'm not telling him I've
only tried to use a tampon once and gave up on it as it
didn't go into my vagina.

"Oh, yeah. My menstruation cycles have been
pretty shaky these days, and… Hey, stop looking at
me like 'OMG! Do I have a crush on a *girl*?'" He lets
out a hearty laughter. Before I started lying through
my teeth, denying his words about having a crush on
him, he continues. "Rest assured, I'm a guy, and so
far, I've never had periods. I just think it'll be nice to

stop the bleeding. Look, we can't exactly take a cab when I'm gushing red liquid like a leaky ketchup bottle. Taxi drivers in Japan are famous for being extra-fussy about keeping their vehicles spotless, right?"

"Right. The driver could kill us if we mess up with the car." I look into my purse and take out a little pouch containing items for just-in-case situations. "I've got a couple of extra-heavy overnight pads."

"Good. Hey, you're also carrying a pair of panty hose. Mind if I use it?"

"Sure, help yourself." At this point, I'm getting used to seeing the unconventional usage of my stuff. "Let me open the packages for you."

"Thanks. I'll buy you brand new stuff later." He takes off his jacket and rolls the right sleeve of his shirt up. Wisecracking like breathing, he puts a maxi pad on his right forearm.

"You don't need to return these little goods to me." I shake my head. "You know, I'd be like an evil bitch if I demand this little stuff back." Especially after what he's done for me. "Um… Thank you so much for rescuing me."

"The pleasure is all mine. It's nice to see your softer side." He winks as he takes off his tie. "Hey, you blew my mind when you got captured by the goons. Who could have guessed playing a little hide and seek would turn out to be a kidnapping?"

"Wait a minute. Did you know I was following you?" My eyes widen. "When did you notice me? Look, I was doing great keeping my profile low, right?"

"I saw you talking like a machine gun at the lobby lounge of the Royal Century," he says casually, compressing his right forearm with the maxi pad.

"Did you notice me at the hotel?" My lips make the shape of the O. "Oh my God. I thought I'd make a great secret agent."

"No. You don't wanna apply for such positions." He shakes his head. "Some people are not cut out to be spies."

"Still, I was lucky to have you watching me. Where were you when the gorillas captured me?"

"I was walking into one of the buildings in the area, and I saw you getting hauled into the van. So I went to the third floor and jumped off the building to stop the vehicle. A brilliant plan, huh?" He winks.

"Excuse me? Did you jump from the third floor?" My eyebrows shoot up north. "Are you crazy? You could have died from the fall!"

"I'm alive." Checking the wound, he changes the maxi pad to a new piece. "On second thought, I might have been a bit reckless, since I ditched my luggage at the entrance of the building. I'm not holding high hopes of recovering my stuff in that neighborhood. Hell, I should have at least moved my passport and wallet into the suit pocket."

"Oh…" I furrow my eyebrows. This doesn't sound good. "Or, you could have used a fanny pack."

"Fanny pack?" He snorts out laughing. "Don't they say you're hilarious?"

"Sometimes." I nod. "Okay, so it's terribly inconvenient to roam around a foreign country without your belongings and passport. You can come to my place tonight. Megu's away for another business trip. Tomorrow, we can contact the U.S. Embassy to arrange a new passport. I also have some clothes you can wear, and they're all brand new. Mom sent me a package about a month ago, making me swear not to sell them, insisting I would need them in the near future."

"What is she? A psychic?"

"Something like that," I say casually. "She can see and hear things most people can't. It's either she had a vision, or Jackie, a ghost of a drag queen, tipped her about the clothes."

"Wow. A ghost of a drag queen? How cool is that?" The corners of his lips quirk up into a smile.

"You really think so?" I turn to him, feeling my heart doing a happy dance. "I thought I scared you, talking about the ghosts and so on. I grew up in Kyoto, Japan's capital of spirituality, so supernatural presence is widely accepted in there, and most of my childhood friends always wanted to say hi to Jackie and Allegra, a fairy attached to this violin." I stroke the violin case sitting next to me. "Osaka is geographically very close to Kyoto, and the local's attitudes toward the supernatural existence are similar to those in Kyoto. Then again, people looked at me like I'd gone insane when I mentioned my non-human friends in Tokyo. Things were about the same in New York, Chicago, London, Paris, and Vienna. So, I don't usually talk about my *invisible* friends with someone I barely know."

"No worries. Just because you have friends invisible to most of us doesn't make you crazy," he assures me. "Hey, are Jackie and Allegra tagging along with us right now? Should I say hi?"

"It'll be nice to say hi to them, but I don't know if they're here." Taking a deep breath, I'm trying my best not to break into tears. I manage to keep my tone breezy as I mention the trouble in Paris and how I met Megu. "Anyway, since then, I've gone totally deaf and blind to ghosts and fairies. About the same time, my musical artistry went on a looong vacation."

For a moment, he's silent. But the next moment, he does a little finger-wave at a blank space in the air. "Hi, Jackie, Allegra, I'm Dante. Nice to see you guys. Actually, I can't see you, but I just wanted to say hi. By the way, Sophie here misses you guys so badly, so you guys might want to work harder so that she can see and chat with you again. How does that sound, huh?"

"Wow…" My jaw drops. "I've never thought

about going persuasive like you."

"Really? If you're having difficulties seeing them, then they should try harder. It's simple like that."

"Maybe. Hey, Jackie, Allegra, did you hear him? I'm listening, so you ladies need to speak up, okay?" To the blank space in the air, I say, "By the way, I managed to play a passable musical scale today during today's lesson. Hopefully, I'm gonna deliver a decent performance for the upcoming concert."

I don't know if Jackie and Allegra are even there close to me, but Dante answers, "Good for you. Things just started to work out." Slightly lifting up the maxi pad, he checks the wound. One of his eyebrows twitches. It's dark, and he's covering the wound itself with a maxi pad. But the shade of his exposed shirtsleeve looks darker, indicating that he's bled a lot.

"Does that hurt?" My voice gets shaky as I ask.

"It's not as bad as it looks. Hey, can you help me wrap it up?" He hands me the tie. "Start from just above the wrist and go upward."

"Sure." I nod. "But, wouldn't it better if you have the arm stitched up? We can just say it's an avocado-related accident."

"Seeing a doctor isn't a good option at the moment. First off, they aren't stupid, and they'll know it's caused by a combat knife. I can picture the cops waiting for me in front of the doctor's office."

"I see…" I nod, but I don't know why he's so desperate to avoid the police. Still, I have a hunch that peppering him with questions regarding his relationship with law enforcement wouldn't lead to a lovely conversation.

"Can you slightly tighten it up?"

"Like this?"

"Yep. Secure the end with the panty hose?" He takes a deep breath as I finish wrapping up. "Thanks."

"Glad to help. Can I clean up your hands?" I take a wad of wipes out of my purse.

"Brilliant. Thanks." Once he's done cleaning his hands, he moves the injured arm and puts on his dark jacket to cover up the bloody shirt. "All right.

No more blood dripping out. Let's go."

Chapter 7

Something cold and sharp touches my throat, prompting me to gasp. Then I feel a huge bump rattling my whole body.

This… can't be… happening… I'm intending to mutter, but I can only make incoherent sounds. I wrinkle my nose as the dusty stench of the van I'd been dragged into. This shouldn't be happening. I was almost kidnapped by some goons, but with Dante's intervention, I was safe. After coming back to Megu's condo together, Dante was sporting fresh clothes and a clean bandage on his arm. We had dinner together in the dining room, chatted a lot, and I honestly enjoyed his company. Everything was going wonderful. How can everything working so beautifully in harmony deteriorate so badly in such a short time?

I'm still hopeful it's only a nightmare, but when I open my eyes and the shabby interior of the dying van jumps in my sight, all of my hopes are shattered. To make it worse, the loud and tasteless voices of Honduran Spanish assaults my hearing.

"What…? Why…?" I mumble, but nobody answers me. All of a sudden, the face of the goon who's previously slashed Dante's arm materializes in front of me. He's holding the knife in death grip, and the blade is tainted with blood. "Wh-wh… where's Dante?"

With an evil grin, he pulls the knife toward him. And the next moment, he stabs me with full force, aiming at my neck.

"Dante… Dante… Where are you…?" The blade slides through my skin and into my throat. I think I should be in agony, but I'm too scared, panicky, and at the same time, confused to feel the pain, and—

"Sophie, Sophie! Wake up!" I hear a voice loud and clear. It's deep, warm, and confident.

"Ah…" I groan as my teeth rattle as strong arms shake my whole body. My head shakes. If I were a baby, I could die from shaken baby syndrome. For the last time before I pass out in death, I've got to complain. Using what's left of my strength, I open my lips. It looks like I've inadvertently opened my eyes. I see the light coming from the doorway. "The goon… The bloody knife… and, he-he-he… slashed my…" I try to explain, but I'm not making any sense. Using only my eyes, I check around me. I'm in my room at Megu's condo, and I see Dante's face close to mine, and he's holding me. I want to have a better look at him, but my vision is blurry. "I… I… I can't see… well…" I whimper between hiccups. "They stabbed my eyes, didn't they?" And I break into a full-blown sob.

"It's okay, Sophie. You're safe. None of the goons can come here. Even if they come, I'm here with you to protect you." He strokes my cheeks with his large hand, repeating, "Don't worry. I'm with you," many times.

My vision clears a little bit. "Dante… Are you… real?" As I ask between sobbing, everything in front of me gets blurry.

"I'm real." Extending one arm, he picks up a box of tissues off the bedside table. "Let's wipe the tears." As he dabs at my eyes, he's using a very soft and gentle tone like he's talking to a little child. With full disclosure, I'm loving it—especially, the part with my vision becoming clearer.

"What…? Oh… maybe my eyes are fine," I mutter, still sniffing.

"Are you feeling better?"

"I guess so." I nod.

"Isn't that great?" He smiles, giving gentle pats on my back. "I heard you shrieking. It got me worried about you."

"Oh my… Did I shriek during a dream? That's so… embarrassing…" I make a face as the situation sinks in. "But… it was so scary. The goon felt so close to me as he tried to stab me." My voice is still shaky. In retrospect, I couldn't do anything but shake when the Hondurans kidnapped me. Even now, I'm just holding onto Dante like a koala. "It felt so real."

"It's okay. Your reaction is normal," he assures me, still keeping me warm in his embrace. "After facing a near-death situation, the bigger shock waves often comes later. Sometimes, you're seriously traumatized in ways you're not even aware of. And you tend to be most vulnerable when you're asleep." Gently stroking my hair, he whispers in my ear.

"Have you been through such a situation?" I ask. "You sound like an expert."

"Oh, yeah." With a light nod, he takes off his T-shirt and reaches for his belt. With the rattle of the metal buckle, he takes it off.

And the next moment, he takes my hand, leading my hand to his back.

"Um… Dante? What are you doing?" I mumble in confusion, but as my fingers move across the skin, I notice some areas feeling significantly rough compared to other parts. It feels like… a scar? And, it's really large.

"Do you feel the scar? I thought I was gonna die when I sustained this injury. I can't tell you much detail, it happened in a helicopter crash. Five people died, and I spent six months in the hospital. Immediately after the first surgery, the doctor told me to brace for the worst, warning that I might never walk on my own legs again. Back in my bedridden days, I used to wake up to my own screaming all the time."

He keeps his tone quiet and matter-of-factly, but my heart aches so badly that I burst into tears.

"I… can't believe you jumped off the third-floor of the building today. What are you… crazy? Why did you take such a huge risk after going through such a serious injury?" I have no right to accuse him, but my motormouth won't stop as I'm bawling like a kid throwing a temper tantrum.

"Come on, Sophie. You don't need to cry." He lets out a low chuckle, stroking my hair ever so gently. "It's been almost year since I got hurt, and my doctor recommends regular exercise to speed up the recovery."

"Is that… supposed to be… a joke?" I stutter, still hiccupping. "What kind of a crazy occupation involves jumping from the third floor?"

"Do you really want to know?" He answers my question with a question, prompting me to groan.

"I… don't know… But it feels like… we're from totally different realms of reality…" I try to smile, but hot tears don't stop rolling down my cheeks. "It's so weird… we're from the same country, and…"

"Oh, yeah. It's weird. But places where women are freely walking around during the nighttime without worrying much about getting killed, raped, or both, are rarer gems in the world." His tone turns serious.

I sniff. "Um… I know it was foolish of me to be kidnapped, but I had no idea Spanish-speaking criminals were roaming around. You know, I've heard about the bad areas, but most of the crimes are vandalizing the vending machines and graffiti…"

"Don't beat yourself up for what's already happened, okay?"

"Okay." I nod, sobbing.

"Good girl." His tone turns light and playful. "So, vandalizing the vending machines? Does that count as a crime?"

"Come on, that's a serious crime! Imagine if you're selling sodas and some goons come destroy the machine and take away the money, would you like that?" I hiccup. Oh my God, I'm crying nonstop.

"No, I'd hate that. I'd be tempted to follow the goons and beat the crap out of them. You're so funny, even when you're crying your eyes out." He chuckles. "By the way, why don't you stop crying? I really hate it when you cry. It makes me sad."

"I'm not crying… for myself…" I press my face against his strong chest. "These are the tears you held back when you were supposed to… cry. So… I'm… shedding all the tears… for the sake of… all the pain, agony, and… f-f-frustration you've… gone through… You can thank me later…"

I'm not making sense, but with a sharp intake of breath, his embrace tightens around me. "Thank you."

Maybe it's just my imagination running wild, but for a moment, his voice sounds like he's choking a bit.

"You're very welcome," I reply in a muffled voice, feeling the warmth of him as we hold onto each other.

If it were one of those new adult romances and not my life, we'd be proceeding to steamy sex—or foreplay with promises of passionate sex, at least. But since I'm lacking expertise in seduction or amour, I spend this moment holding onto him and soaking his brand-new T-shirt with my tears. And all the while, he keeps on stroking my back like he's consoling a fussy child.

After a while, the tears start to dry, my breathing goes back to normal, and I'm still cuddling him. While cherishing the warmth and presence of Dante and listening to his heart beat, I have this sudden, strange desire in me. A desire that drives the fingers of my left hand to dance, my right hand to hold the bow and swirl, and my heart to start... singing? Also, the third movement of the Violin Concerto in D Major, by Tchaikovsky, is blasting in my head.

Oh my God... My eyes widen and my heart is beating faster. I want to hold my violin, stroke its deep amber-colored surface, and if possible, I want to play the instrument... to make music! Honestly, I've never felt this excited for the mere imagination of the violin in many, many years. The excitement. The thrill. And, the drive. Some may even call it an orgasm—except, I'm lacking in sexual experience. It's like my very first encounter with Allegra and the Guarneri violin.

I was three, at Granddaddy Dan's house party at his Upper East Side mansion. Just like any of the other parties, it was boring for a child. He had a string orchestra over, and I liked it. While the orchestra were having a break, my parents were distracted by some of the guests, so I snuck out and approached the podium to get a close look at the musical instruments.

Then I found this apple-sized lady, with see-through wings on her back, sitting at the edge of a violin case, with her arms crossed and legs dangling. I didn't hesitate to run to her, saying, "Hi! I'm Sophie. Today, my granddaddy's having a party! I hope you're enjoying it. What's your name?" With her eyebrows going up north, she said, "Can you see me?" adding, "I'm Allegra. It's a pleasure to meet you, Sophie." With a smile, she said, "Why don't you try playing the violin I'm attached to?" and the lid of the case popped open. In retrospect, the instrument was too big for a three-year-old, as it was a full-size violin, but I held the instrument and the bow, and started making sounds, following her instruction.

It didn't take long for the adults to find me playing the beginning of the violin solo part for Tchaikovsky's Violin Concerto. When I found myself surrounded by a horde of adults, I thought they were mad at me. I cried a little in an attempt to get away, but Mr. Edelmann, then-owner of the violin, lowered himself to meet my eyes, applauding. "Sophie, I'm so impressed. You're an amazing musician!" he said, and I giggled with an, "I know!"

I had no idea what I was talking about, but according to Mom, I used to declare "I know!" every time I opened my mouth back then.

It turned out that Mr. Edelmann was looking for a buyer of his Guarneri piece—a family heirloom passed down for centuries—to pay for the medical bill for his grandson. As much as he wanted to help his teenage grandchild fighting a rare form of cancer, his heart was crying. At the bottom of his heart, he hated to say goodbye forever to the violin.

Even though he couldn't communicate with the fairies, Allegra was well-aware of his situation. She had no choice but to follow Mr. Edelmann's decision, but she hated the uncertainty with her future. She might end up in the hands of a collector who'd lock her up in a temperature and humidity-controlled room for centuries. On top of all that, she liked Mr. Edelmann, and she was hoping to see him once in a while even after separating from him. When she was musing what to do, yours truly—the granddaughter of this extravagant party's host—appeared in front of her.

Anyway, everything worked in harmony for everyone. Mr. Edelmann got the money, his grandson quickly and fully recovered, and Allegra got to meet her previous owner regularly. I had a new fairy friend, and a superb and patient professor of the violin. Granddaddy Dan, who purchased the violin, had something new—his granddaughter's musical genius—to brag about at parties and salons.

I want to play the violin… At least, I want to try. My spine straightens up.

"What's up, Sophie? Don't worry. You're safe now." Dante strokes my back. "You want to go to sleep?"

"I'm okay. Thanks." Giving him a gentle pat on the shoulder, I look at him. "Can you possibly listen to me play the violin? It may sound weird, but right now, it feels like I can make decent music. I want to play the violin for you. At least, I wanna try."

"Fabulous." He smiles. "All right. Grab your instrument and try it. I'm listening."

"Sure." Stepping down to the floor, I switch on the light and pick up the violin case. As I put on the chin rest and shoulder rest, I'm smiling. My fingers aren't shaking as I tune up the violin. "I'm ready."

"I can't wait to listen to your concert." He sits up.

"Oh, relax." I clear my throat. "Just one thing. I'd appreciate it if you don't snort out laughing, even if my performance turns out to be below your expectations."

"No worries. Focus on your music and enjoy." Now he's sounding like Mr. Edelmann.

"I will." After bowing to my audience, I start playing YMCA. When I make the first passage in the right tune and pitches, Dante gives me a thumbs-up. I selected this piece mostly because it's less complex than, say, Paganini Caprice No.24, or La Campanella.

"Bravo!" He applauds when I finish the piece. "Who said you can't play the violin? You've just delivered an amazing performance."

"Thanks! Oh, you don't wanna clap so vigorously. You're injured, remember?"

"I almost forgot. Your music has soothing effects." He winks.

"Thank you. The next piece is Caprice No. 24, Niccolo Paganini," I announce. "When you get sleepy, don't hesitate to lie down and go to sleep."

As I continue to play the violin, my arms, fingers, and whole body feel warm, energized, and alive. Oh, yeah. I'm on a roll. I keep on playing the instrument, in the medley style. When I finish Caprice No. 24, I proceed with Czardas by Monti, La Campanella, Caprice No. 1, a little excerpt from Tchaikovsky's Violin Concerto, and so much more. When I realize it's already late at night, I slow down, playing softer pieces like Meditation from Thais. While I'm playing Thais, I notice Dante nodding off, and I'm so happy to see him that way. Good music excites the audience, and the better music relaxes the crowd.

When I finish with Air on the G-string, composed by J. S. Bach, he's sound asleep.

"Thank you for listening to my performance!" I bow, whispering gratitude to my Guarneri, Dante, and every existence in the universe. "Thank you so much, Allegra, and Jackie."

As soon as I'm done returning the violin in the case and to the regular place, I snuggle in my bed—next to Dante, cuddling him. Mmm, he's like a big teddy bear, and I'm loving this moment. His presence gives me a huge feeling of relaxation, and it takes mere seconds for me to fall asleep.

Intermezzo

Light spills into the living room, spreading all over the area as Dante opens up the curtain.

It's been three years since his last visit to Japan. Every time he comes to this country, the blindingly bright sunbeam reminds him of the nation's nickname "the land of the rising sun." Fifteen years ago, he left this country for good, vowing never to return. Ironically, his job kept on sending him back on a regular basis. Still, he never took time to meet Esq. Megumi Nakamura.

With a bottled water in one hand, he walks toward the suit jacket hanging over the back of the sofa. After taking a few sips of water, he reaches for the inner pocket. Immediately, his hand comes out with a little booklet with a red cover, Japan Passport printed in gold letters. Putting the bottle on the coffee table, he flips through the booklet until his fingers reaches the page with the page with the photo and personal data. The man in the photograph looks back at Dante with penetrating eyes.

The passport is real, and the man in the photo is Dante himself. Kento Nakamura, his name as a Japanese citizen, appears next to his American name, Dante Walker. The entry stamp to Japan at KIX appears on the next page. It's the only stamp on this passport since he hasn't used the regular passport for more than a decade. Born in Princeton, he's a U.S. citizen, but since he hasn't renounced Japanese citizenship yet, he has two passports. This time, he elected to use the regular passport to enter Japan. Given the personal nature of this trip, using his official passport felt wrong on so many levels.

"Spending a night at my mother's place with her assistant?" he mutters to himself. "Can life get more surreal than this?"

It was supposed to be a simple errand. Flying to Osaka, returning the $300,000 check to Megumi Nakamura, and going back to the U.S.

A young man and woman, both coming from wealthy families, met at Princeton University, hooked up, and got pregnant with Dante. That's how his family started. Robert Walker, his father, was the heir to the Walker Group, one of the biggest real estate companies on the East Coast. Megumi Nakamura, his mother, was an heiress to Japan's trading giant. The Walkers celebrated their marriage and the newly conceived child while the Nakamuras pushed for the termination of the pregnancy and separation. Megumi chose Robert and Dante over her family, and they started a new family.

In the beginning, the Walkers were happy, but the bliss started to crack as soon as they relocated to Japan due to a family emergency on Megumi's side. After years of endless fighting between his parents, it was over. Dante came back to the U.S. with his father, mostly because he hated his mother's guts. Back then, she was nothing but a heartless corporate bitch to him, with no compassion or interest in her husband and son.

The $300,000 check has been the symbol of the family relationship in the past fifteen years. A week after divorce, his mother sent the money to his father, citing it as alimony and child support. His father sent it back to her, and the money has been moving like a silly ping-pong game.

Last month, Megumi visited Robert, dropping

the check on his desk. In order to return the check to the sender, Dante came to Japan as a messenger. He'd been avoiding getting involved with his parents' issues, but this time, he did. He was still on convalescent leave following the helicopter-crush injury. He had time to kill, so he decided to give a shot and meet his mother.

The reunion couldn't get more awkward.

"I know I'm not entitled to lecture you like a mother, but please take good care of yourself. If anything happens to you, the whole Walker family will be shattered," was how she opened up the conversation.

"Did you hear something about me?" he had to ask. "Dad is supposed to know nothing about it."

"I have a friend from Princeton with the U.S. Navy. You were seriously hurt, right? I had a call from him, informing that you'd been discharged from the hospital, walking on your own legs. I cried." Her voice was slightly trembling. He could only shrug.

A Princeton graduate in his fifties should be an admiral, or someone of higher rank. Dante has always made it crystal clear that the only time the

Navy can contact his family will be to notify them of his death. He didn't want anyone to see him in his worst shape.

"Speaking of crying, don't break Dad's heart." Braving himself, he kept his tough façade. "Women practically throw themselves at him, but he's never remarried. You know what that means?"

"I'll try." Her tone was cool and composed, but a flicker of emotion crossed her eyes.

"Let me make this clear. Drop the case with Kakubeni Holdings as this matter involves a Honduran cartel. I also caught a rumor that Kakubeni will proceed with the transaction as soon as the bad hombres strike you from the picture."

It wasn't a happy sight to see his mother's complexion turning as white as Mozzarella, but at least he made his point. Also, he got to slip the check in the jacket pocket of her pantsuit.

A week later, a text from Megumi, saying *I now know this case needs urgent attention. Thanks for the tip!* came in Dante's inbox. As if to avoid Dante getting in her way, she sent her assistant who knew absolutely nothing about the case or her employer's relationship with him.

Even worse, his mother used the check, again, to have it her way. Add that she sent her assistant like the ace of spades—to distract him so that she'd hop on the plane without her son getting in the way.

A personal assistant? Seriously? He lets out a sigh as Sophie's face pops up in his mind. When he noticed the snooping eyes, he went for the watcher's back. His moves came out of caution, but the ogler turned out to be a petite girl who is too adorable to call a woman. On second thought, he couldn't help but noticing the hidden allure under her fluffy, cotton candy-like façade when he touched her.

She was the kind of a woman he's never been involved before. Swiftly, he stepped aside from her before getting too enchanted by her—or at least, so he thought.

Who could have imagined I'd meet her again? With a mere thought of Sophie, a corner of his lips quirk up to form a lopsided grin. At first, he regarded her as a juvenile woman with attitude, but he was wrong. As much as she's soft and fluffy, he could feel the rock solidness of her core. At least, she's strong enough to show her vulnerability and inner conflict with him—which has never been his strong suit.

When he raises his arms to stretch his spine, a flicker of amusement crosses his face. This morning, his lower back feels so light and… good. Since the helicopter crash, even after a series of successful surgeries, a dull ache and heaviness in his lower back remained. He had started to accept the discomfort as a part of his life, however, the pain seems to be taking a leave.

"Wow…" he mutters to himself. "It's true about music therapy working like magic?" Tilting his head, he can't help sounding like he's asking a question than making a statement. He remembers wishing to punch the guy playing the same tune in loop with the violin when he tried music therapy before. Back then, Dante was still paralyzed and fragile, and he couldn't even stand. At that time, all he could do was curse under his breath.

Last night, when Sophie played the violin, he was taken by surprise. He totally underestimated her talent with the violin. After listening to her story at the park, he was still thinking that music would be something like a hobby for a rich and pampered kid. But when she started to play the instrument, she was playing as if she was channeling with the super-virtuoso Niccolo Paganini himself. Every sound she produced was beyond beautiful, making exquisite music. Her performance didn't sound like coming from someone who played the violin for the first time after a year-long hiatus. Honestly, Dante wants to strangle the son of a bitch responsible for Sophie's loss of her music for such a long time. Dante is well aware that the SOB has been dead for a while, but it's always tempting to beat the crap out of the bad guys.

When the landline phone in the living room rings, he takes it immediately, before Sophie wakes up.

"How is Sophie? Is she safe?" Nakamura demands before he even utters "Hello?"

He was expecting this call from his mother. Even though Sophie was worrying that she'd been unable to catch her employer on the road, finding a person in the United States is easy for Dante. This time, he hired someone to find Megumi, and notify her that Sophie had been assaulted.

"So far, she's safe. The assailants were seven Hispanic goons talking in Honduran accents." As he speaks, a gasp comes from the other end. "Shocking, huh? Is that because you're worried about your employee who claims to be your lover? Or…?"

Dante takes a deep breath as he braces himself for any crazy revelation.

It's been ten days since he met Sophie for the time. He attempted to disappear from the young woman's life, but when he saw her at the hotel's lobby lounge with her friends, he purposefully showed up in her sight.

He knew Sophie was tailing him, but continued the little hide-and-seek. At that point, he didn't expect her to get kidnapped.

He had to get her back while the van was in the alley as the rescue plan was going to be much more complex when they went into the busy main road. He had no time to check the Hondurans' weapons and skills, so ambushing them was the only realistic option.

The truth is, he's been secretly checking around Sophie after hearing about her living arrangement with Nakamura. Having found no imminent threat at her home and workplace, Dante assessed the risk to Sophie's personal safety as minimal.

In retrospect, his judgment was biased, and he knows what caused that. He's been having a lingering question about his mother's relationship with Sophie, which is far from romantic. And the doubt has been snowballing ever since he saw Dan Rowling's personal card slipping out of Sophie's purse.

"You've been seeing Dan Rowling, the COB of USCAB, for decades, am I correct? Back then, I was too young to fathom things like that... Hell, never mind. When I was a teenager, I came across a gossip article on the close tie between you and Mr. Rowling. Is that the reason why you're living with her, and taking care of her like your own daughter?"

Despite trying his best to keep his tone emotion-free, bitterness oozes out of his voice. When Sophie was born, he had just relocated to Kyoto with his family. Ironically, it was the same timing as the bond of the Walker family started to crack. His father, who left the Walker Group to join his wife's side of family company, was having a hell of a time trying to adjust to a different corporate culture in a foreign country, and his mother was too busy running the company. In a nutshell, Dante's previously happy childhood being ruined was an understatement.

Now that Megumi Nakamura is back in legal circle, he can imagine that becoming a corporate shark wasn't her favorite lifestyle. Also, he can think of her conflict and confusion in her home country, juggling with her duties as the CEO of a huge company, her husband showing the signs of depression, and her son turning more rebellious by the day.

"Tell," Dante says through the gritted teeth. "I'm ready for anything."

If it turns out what he's thinking, he must stop being attracted to Sophie. Whatever it takes.

A deep sigh comes from the other end, followed by "Dante, did you hit your head in the chopper crush?"

"What?"

"I'm just wondering if it's one of the trauma-related aftereffects."

"Don't even think about talking your way out of my question. I'm not a kid you can easily distract anymore."

"I'm not trying to distract you. It's just, I'm simply impressed with your overly wild imagination. You should seriously consider writing fiction." Megumi chuckles. "On second thought, I'm *a little* shocked with your nonsense. Listen to me, young man. Do you seriously think I had time *and* energy to have an affair with another man, get pregnant, and give birth to a baby girl while juggling CEO duties, attempting to smooth up the relationship between my husband, the Japanese corporate culture, and my picky parents? Oh, don't forget my extra-rebellious son who couldn't stop picking a fight at every school he'd attended and kicked out of. Wow, I must be some kind of a Wonder Woman to you. I am so flattered."

"Shit," Dante curses under his breath, grimacing. *Why am I arguing with a fucking lawyer?*

"When Sophie was born at Mount Sinai, New York, Dan sent me an email with the photos of the baby girl. He sent that particular photo to every friend in his business circle, so I was one of many recipients. I still remember the moment I got it. I was in Kyoto, at the hospital's waiting room while they took the X-rays of your hand. Honestly, I had to think hard about things like, 'Did I commit something horrible in my previous life?' After all, when Dan was celebrating the birth of his first grandchild, I was worrying sick about my own son who broke his fist by punching an older kid in another fight. I was biting my lower lip, wondering if that was the way karma punished me. The caption on the baby Sophie's photo said, *'Hi! I'm Sophie, the first girl Rowling born in more than a century! Nice to meet you. Ooh-hoo!'* Oh, did I mention Sophie is the spitting image of her mom, Mandy Rowling?"

"Oh, yeah?" is all Dante can say.

Megumi continues, "If you don't believe me, I'll show you the photos and the doctor's note with the date, time, and everything taken at the hospital in Kyoto. I can even ask Dan to send me a copy of the video when…"

"Fine." Dante cuts in on his mother in midsentence. "I don't need the photos and so on.

Um… thanks?"

Epilogue: Violinist's Prelude into the Storm

Somewhere in the distance, the phone is ringing.

Gotta get up and answer the phone... My right hand twitches, but the phone stops ringing. The silence lulls me back to sleep, and I'm loving it.

My brain is shifting between asleep and awake statuses. In between, I'm giddy, recalling what happened previously. After my decent violin performance, I periodically saw nightmarish dreams featuring the goons attempting to kidnap me. Every time I grunted and whimpered, Dante held me tighter, whispering sweetly in my ear and steering me back to sleep. As I repeated the process, Dante joined the cast of my nightmares as the hero who always rescued me. And then, the nightmares turned into sweet dreams...

"Sophie... Hey, why are you giggling?" Dante asks in a sweet tone that reminds me of the chocolate he gave me on our first encounter. As I'm enjoying a delicious memory, he strokes my back.

"Um… It smells… amazing…" I mumble, opening a slit of an eye and sniffing the air. "Mmm… coffee? Ohh… my dreams just keep on getting juicier and happier…" I mumble, getting giddier.

"I'd hate to interrupt you in the middle of enjoying sweet dreams, but it's real." Dante's voice caresses my ears. "Why don't you wake up?"

I open my eyes, expecting to see the same old ivory-colored ceiling of my room. Instead, Dante's handsome face comes into my view.

"Good morning, Sophie." He gives me a peck on my cheek. "How's my virtuoso feeling this morning?"

"Good morning," I reply, with a half of my brain still asleep.

"Come quick. Coffee and eggs are waiting for you."

"Wow." My eyes widen. "Did you make breakfast for me? Oh, my."

"Oh, it's nothing fancy. Making coffee, scrambling eggs, and throwing bread in the toaster. Oh, and I had the help of the coffee machine." He winks.

I notice he's looking pretty freshened up, the five o'clock shadow on his face having disappeared. I make a mental note to thank my mom for including an electric shaver in the package she sent to me.

The curtains are already open. I squint as the violently bright summer sun spills into the room. This morning, Dante's hair looks a lighter shade of blond. Then I realize I'm in pajamas, without makeup, probably sporting bedhead.

"Um... sorry. I should have made breakfast for the guest..." I mumble, looking away from him in hopes of hiding my unfashionable mess. To make matters worse, the pajamas I'm wearing have Gudetama the Lazy Egg all over the fabric. Not that there's anything wrong with the yellowness or the lazy egg, but... why did I choose such a childish garment? Besides that, after the crazy crying last night, I have a hunch that my face is a blotchy mess.

"No worries. I'm not a freeloader. Isn't it best for the early bird to fix the breakfast? So, let's go and eat before the food gets cold."

"Brilliant," I say, feeling Dante really close to

me. "I'll join you once I'm finished getting dressed… Oh!" I yelp as he scoops me up from the bed.

"All right. I can see you're a polite and tidy person, but sometimes, it's fun to break all the rules. How about starting off with eating breakfast in pajamas?" Laughing, he carries me toward the dining room.

"I promise to eat breakfast in pajamas, but can I go to the bathroom first?" I've got things to do before eating breakfast. Did you know that you have gazillions of bacteria in your mouth immediately after waking up? I've got to wash my face and brush my teeth, and at least comb my hair.

"Sure." He changes direction and lowers me in front of the toilet. "Take your time."

"Wow." My eyes widen when I come to the dining room to see meticulously presented breakfast plates of scrambled eggs, sausages, and a salad of fresh vegetables lined up on the dining table. The butter is melting on top of the toasted bread, and the scent of freshly brewed coffee is to die for. "Everything looks and smells so delicious. Dante, you rock at cooking."

"I'll take that as a compliment." He smiles, placing a coffee in front of me. "I like this mug. It matches your pajamas. So adorable."

"Oh…" I look at the mug, and then at my pajamas. I can only manage to mumble. What was I thinking? Why did I choose something as unsexy as an egg yolk who can't stop muttering "Meh… Mmm… I need a shot of soy sauce…" while sitting on his egg white?

"Relax." With Megu's cool and classy mug featuring the Waikiki Beach in one hand, Dante sits next to me, to my left. "It's yours, right? If it belongs to Nakamura, my jaw's gonna drop."

"Come on. Megu looked lovely when we visited Gudetama's café previously."

"Seriously?" He leans in, his bluish-green eyes focused on me.

"Um… Can you stop staring at me? This is getting embarrassing. You know. I'm in pajamas, I haven't put on makeup, and my hair is still messy…"

"I'd prefer tasting your skin than licking foundation and lipstick. By the way, don't you think bedhead is sexier compared to some impeccably-styled hairdo?" He reaches for my hair with his left hand, putting the mug on the table.

My heart jumps as I feel his nimble fingers caressing my hair, but then I notice he's not using his right hand, which is closer to me. "Wait a minute, you're in pain, aren't you?" Leaning toward him, I try to have a better look at his injured arm. "You shouldn't have lifted me up…"

The distance between us closes and his lips touch one of my earlobes. When he bites my ear ever so lightly, the mug in my hand almost gets knocked off.

Catching the falling mug in a smooth move, he looks into my eyes. "Actually, there's a thing with which your help will be much appreciated. But maybe you'd say no?"

"If you say something like 'Can I have one of your kidneys?' I can't give you an immediate yes, but…" I think hard and continue, "I'll do my best. I can't thank you enough for what you did for me last night."

"No worries, I'm not even thinking of asking you for your organs." He chuckles. "By the way, thanks for a great concert last night. I didn't know you were such an awesome violinist. There's something about the sound coming from your music. When I closed my eyes, it felt as if every musical note you produced was singing and sparkling on its own."

"Really?" I perk up. "Thank you sooo much! You just gave me the biggest compliment for a musician."

"A compliment? No, it's my honest opinion." He shakes his head. "What was Nakamura thinking? Hiring you as her personal assistant?"

"Megu took me under her wings when I forgot how to play the violin, and she's been great to me. You can't badmouth her."

"Okay. I might be a bit too harsh on her. I only know her as the CEO of her family business." He adds, "That was before she opened her law firm. I think she got her softer side back after returning to practicing law. She was like an evil bitch when she was the CEO."

"An evil bi...?" I hold my tongue before fully parroting him. "I can't imagine it."

"It's just my personal opinion."

"So, you and Megu have a long-standing history, I assume?"

"You can say that. Basically, I'm the middleman between her and my client who has also known her for a long time."

"I see." After a moment's pause, I say, "I trust you."

"Good. So, can I expect your help?"

"Sure."

"Good girl." Displaying a sweet smile, he indicates the table. "Shall we start eating?"

"Yes, let's. Oh my God…" As I take a bite of scrambled eggs. My eyes widen. The eggs taste so fluffy, creamy, and melt away on my tongue. It's so true about yummy food making you happy. I think I'm grinning like a total idiot, but I'm busy enjoying great food. "This is sooo delicious. Thank you so much."

"The pleasure is all mine."

* * *

When we're finished eating, he takes me to the bathroom. Just like any home in Japan, there are only the bathtub and shower stall in the bathroom, adjacent to the washroom.

"So, I've managed to shave, but getting the wound wet isn't in my best interest, right? Then again, it's hard to wash myself using just one hand—especially, when the good one happens to be my non-dominant hand. That's why I need your help." Taking off all the clothes he's wearing, he goes toward the shower and gestures for me to come.

"Wait a minute. I-I-I… wasn't expecting to do… this in the morning?" I stutter, sounding more like questioning than making a statement.

"You know what? It's normal to take a shower in the morning. So, you don't trust me… after getting my arm slashed while keeping your head from saying goodbye forever to your body," he mutters in a low voice, prompting me to feel like such a callous person with no sense of gratitude.

"Of course, I trust you, Dante! It's just… I didn't expect to help you when you're… um… I mean… naked!"

"Can you wash someone who's fully clothed?" He tilts his head, giving me a quizzical look.

"No…" He has a point. Taking a deep breath, I make up my mind. "Okay, I don't need to undress myself, right? What I'll be doing is washing you."

"Of course, you can keep the clothes on. Still, you might get wet."

"I know." Throwing my pajamas into the washing machine with one hand, I grab a pink terrycloth bathrobe from the cabinet. I don't forget to secure the bathrobe with a belt around my hips as I throw it on over my underwear.

As I move, I glance at the mirror in the corner of my eyes. Inside the mirror, my cheeks are pink, and I'm looking so happy…

I clear my throat. "O-o-kay… So, I'm gonna wis-was-wash you… Ju-just keep on facing the wall." I'm desperate to stay calm and cool, but my tongue is so uncooperative.

Taking another deep breath, I go in the bathroom and take the shower hose off the hook. In front of me is Dante's broad back. He's sitting on an acrylic shower stool.

After turning on the shower until the water

gets hot enough, I wet his broad back. "Is the temperature good? Tell me if it's too hot or too cold," I say, reaching for a sponge on the shelf by the shower hook.

"The temperature is perfect."

"Good." I soak the sponge with water and lather a bar of soap till the bubbles fly.

I start with his shoulder and move down to his back. When I'm washing the area under the scapula, my hands stop moving. There's a round-shaped scar. *Is this a healed gunshot wound?* I wonder, but I can't bring myself to ask this question. What's more, he has so many scars across his back. As I go down to his lower back, I suck in the air, noticing the huge scar he mentioned last night. This one runs down to his butt.

I recall him mentioning the helicopter crash, five deaths, and the surgeries. It looks like he was telling the truth.

"Sophie, when you touch me like this, you're turning me on."

"What? Oh…" My eyes widen, noticing that I'm stroking his lower back using my palms. "Sorry about that. I got distracted by the scar on your lower back. Well… I mean, are you really sure you're good?" I ask sheepishly.

For a moment, he's silent. "If you ask me, I'm not really okay."

"Oh my God. Are you in pain? Where does it hurt?"

"Yeah, it feels somewhat tight in the front…"

"In the front? Did you get injured there as well? If you have pain, is it better to ice it?" I'm so worried about him so I run my hand across his hipbone. I don't feel the scars, but when I reach the front, something hard touches my finger. Without giving it much thoughts, I clasp it. "What is this…? WHAT?" My monologue turns into an exclamation.

Oh, yes. I didn't go to medical school, but I don't need medical license to deduce the name of the *thing* in my hand. *Is this… even real? Geez, this is sooo huuuuge!* My lips form the shape of an O as I mentally shriek.

"Holy crap. It's been a while since someone touched me so seductively. Hey, Sophie, what do you say if I ask you to be mine right here, right now?"

"Dante... Does that mean you're…? Oh my God! I'm so sorry! I didn't mean to…" Releasing his private part, I yank my arm toward me. And the next thing I know, I'm grabbing the diverter valve of the shower. Cold water falls on me at full blast. "Noooo!"

"Come on, Sophie. Chill. You're bathing in cold water before washing me." He reaches for the faucet and stops the water.

"I'm sorry…" I mumble, completely soaked in cold water.

As for Dante, he's as wet as me. As the soap bubbles flow into the drain, he lets out a low chuckle. "You're a slow learner, aren't you?"

I wish I were dead, and I'm serious. Just a moment ago, things were getting so romantic, and his tone was seductive. But again, my clumsiness overpowered the potential of romance!

I'm on the verge of tears, but isn't it lame to cry at this timing? As I try to blink away the tears, Dante's finger touches my chin, and in a smooth move, he lifts up my face.

I'm watching the bluish green of his eyes coming closer to me.

My lips are parted.

I'm wondering whether to call his name, or close my eyes.

Before I can decide, my lips are sealed with his. *Oh my God... He's kissing me!*

For a moment I'm taken by surprise, but then I start to smile.

My mind is set. I'm going to let the flow and passion sweep us away, and I love my plan.

To be continued to ***Witch's Guide to Romantic Comedy: Capturing Dante: https://amzn.to/3oGhanq***

About the author

Hi! My name is Lotta Smith. I've been writing paranormal cozy mysteries for a while. Lately, I just discovered the enchanting world of romance, and I'm loving it. It's

I'm hard at work writing new books.

Paranormal in Manhattan Mysteries:

https://www.amazon.com/gp/product/B07KJK96RF

Witch's Guide to Haunted Properties: Los Angeles:

https://www.amazon.com/gp/product/B07VW7QZKM

PI Assistant Extraordinaire Mysteries:

Book 1: Ghostly Murder:

http://amzn.to/2O4aWJ4

Book 2: Immortal Eyes:

http://amzn.to/1T4DKC3

Book 3: Deadly Vision:

http://amzn.to/1og0Pp9

Also, there's a bundle of 3 books available…

Confessions of the Assistant Extraordinaire:

amzn.to/1R3GaO6

Printed in Great Britain
by Amazon

80739790R10108